Murder on Sunset Boulevard

Murder on Sunset Boulevard

Sister in Crime / LA Chapter

Edited By

ROCHELLE KRICH

MICHAEL MALLORY

LISA SEIDMAN

Top Publications, Ltd.
Dallas, Texas

Murder on Sunset Boulevard

A Top Publications Paperback

First Edition

Top Publications, Ltd.
12221 Merit Drive, Suite 750
Dallas, Texas 75251

ISBN#: 1-929976-19-4

Library of Congress Control Number 2002107294

Printed in the United States of America

Contents

INTRODUCTION:
MURDER ON SUNSET BOULEVARD

by Rochelle Krich

Sunset Boulevard—famous and infamous, grand and evocative—is the setting for murder in this collection of twelve new mystery stories by Los Angeles-based writers. Just as Sunset changes its character as it winds through neighborhoods from downtown L.A. to the Pacific, the stories vary in tone and style. Each presents a unique perspective of Sunset. All were written by members of the Los Angeles Chapter of Sisters in Crime, a local organization part of a national network that has had a profound impact on mystery writing over the past decade.

Sisters in Crime was formed in 1986 by a group of female writers who had become friends and shared the concern that mystery writing was considered the domain of tough-talking American men and a few noteworthy Englishwomen, an outdated perception being reinforced by newspaper reviews. Statistics verified that reviewers covered fewer mysteries written by women than by men, despite the fact that they sold as well, or often better, than new books by men.

Led by Sara Paretsky, the friends formed Sisters in Crime to celebrate the work of women in the mystery field and educate the public (reviewers included) about their history and accomplishments. Novelist Marilyn Wallace solidified the mission of the organization as editor of an anthology of short stories entitled *Sisters in Crime*. The book's success led to four subsequent volumes, and the series, now reprinted around the world, has introduced readers to an array of women writers and demonstrated that mystery anthologies continue to have great commercial appeal.   Over the past decade, Sisters in Crime has flourished. This supportive network provides information, helps publicize its authors and encourages new voices.

In 1989 I was one of those voices. I learned of Sisters in Crime at a parent-teacher conference. I was the teacher; the parent, who knew I was writing a mystery, mentioned that her friend Phyllis Miller was founder and first president of the Los Angeles Chapter. Perhaps I might find it interesting? At my first meeting, held in the former Mysterious Bookshop West (since relocated to Westwood and renamed The Mystery Bookstore), I sat at the back of the long, narrow, book-filled room and marveled at the serendipity that had brought me to this gathering of writers, booksellers, and readers, all of whom shared my passion for mysteries.

I was warmly welcomed by Phyllis and other chapter founding members—writers Wendy Hornsby, Serita Stevens, Gerry Maddren, Carol Russell Law and Anita Zelman, and bookseller Terry Baker of Mystery Annex at Small World Books. They took me under their wing. I learned about the importance of networking at mystery conventions like Malice Domestic and Bouchercon, where you can attend panels on craft and promotion and meet editors and agents and writers who, if they like your work, may give you a jacket blurb. I learned how to pitch a query letter to an agent and how to set up book signings if your publisher doesn't do it for you. I learned police procedure from an LAPD detective, forensics from a representative of the coroner's office, criminal law from a prosecutor.

When my agent sold my first book, Terry Baker hosted my debut signing. At a San Diego bookstore event that I learned of through my chapter, I talked with an editor who would later buy my Jessie Drake series, and I first met the editor of my new Molly Blume series at Malice Domestic. At that first Sisters in Crime meeting in 1989, I didn't know what Bouchercon was or how to spell it. Two years later, when the convention was held in Pasadena, my first mystery, *Where's Mommy Now?*, won the award for Best Paperback Original. Without the support and encouragement of Sisters in Crime, I don't think I would have been standing at that podium.

I had the pleasure and honor of serving as a Los Angeles Chapter president, and I've been gratified to watch the chapter grow. Today monthly meetings are held at the South Pasadena Public Library, and the chapter continues to recruit provocative and illuminating guest speakers, to share information about writing opportunities and to further the goals of the national organization. It has a diverse membership of women and men, which includes working writers, aspiring writers, teachers, librarians, book dealers, film and TV professionals and mystery fans.

Over the years, SinC/LA has undertaken many ambitious projects. The group hosted a "Guide to Hollywood" half-day presentation featuring television producers and writers at Bouchercon '91 and co-sponsored a special evening with Sara Paretsky at the Writers Guild of America. It created a Speakers Bureau, which promotes and increases the visibility of chapter members while providing entertaining and educational programs to the community. More recently, SinC/LA launched "No Crime Unpublished," a biennial conference for new writers, and published *Murder by 13, A Deadly Dozen,* and two volumes of *Desserticide,* a cookbook that pairs dessert recipes with tongue-in-cheek advice for the would-be murderer.

Which brings us to Murder on Sunset Boulevard, the third anthology of short stories that SinC/LA has produced to exhibit the talents of many of its members. Stories were submitted anonymously and selected on the basis of characterization, originality, mystery plot and voice.   Several authors featured in this anthology are making their print debuts.   Others are experienced professionals. All are writers we believe you'll enjoy.

FOREWORD: INTO THE SUNSET

By Michael Mallory

It has been called the "Boulevard of Dreams." It ranks as the fourth longest street among the more than ten thousand that make up the sprawling tangle of Los Angeles. It has remained a focal point of commerce and culture through every decade of the city's history, from its beginnings as an Indian foot path, long before European explorers ever set boot tracks in the California soil, to its present incarnation as a ribbon of concrete. If Los Angeles were to lay claim to its own indigenous "Mother Road," it would certainly be Sunset Boulevard.

To most of the world, "Sunset Boulevard" evokes moody, monochrome images of desperate lives played out against the decaying splendor of old Hollywood, as seen in Billy Wilder's classic 1950 film of the same name (which, in a typical example of Hollywood deceit, used the Getty mansion on *Wilshire* Boulevard for its exterior scenes). But to Angelenos, the diverse and teeming masses that make up the explosion of life called L.A., Sunset Boulevard is something entirely different.

The real Sunset Boulevard is a virtual blueprint of the city, a twenty-five mile east/west thoroughfare that starts out on the west edge of present day downtown, near the original *pueblo de Los Angeles*, established in 1781, and ends at the shore of the Pacific Ocean. The path of

Sunset Boulevard cuts through the strata of Los Angeles like a scalpel, revealing every social, economic, ethnic, even topographical layer the city has to offer.

To drive Sunset Boulevard is to truly experience Los Angeles in all its many facets, faces and facades, from the day-to-day realities of once-fashionable, now gritty Angelino Heights, to the unreal, cosmetically buoyant glitz of Beverly Hills. It is a corridor from which the doors of such diverse sub-communities as Chinatown, Little Tokyo, Mexican Olvera Street, Hollywood, UCLA and Bel Air are easily opened.

With the possible exception of New York's "Great White Way"—Broadway — no street anywhere so captures and characterizes its city as Sunset Boulevard. And no other street knows so much about its residents: their glories, their failings, their triumphs and their tragedies—but most of all, their secrets.

A dozen of those secrets are here in this book, stories of the City of Angels illuminated by some of Southern California's finest mystery writers, from the Los Angeles Chapter of Sisters in Crime.

They are waiting to take you on a journey. They are pulling the car up to the curb, opening the door, and beckoning you into the passenger seat. Get in; you're in good hands. Sit back and enjoy the ride.

Just bear this in mind: this road can be dangerous.

CLOSING TIME

By Dana Kouba

"Oughta get yourself outta here, Meg." Earl tossed back his shot, set the glass on the scarred wooden bar, and washed the bourbon down with a swig of beer. "Probably get a few hundred thou for the building, little extra for the business, make yourself a nice start somewhere. Hell, you're still young. No, don't look at me like that. Forty-two ain't old. Artie have any insurance?"

Meg Ortiz hefted an aluminum beer keg into place beneath the bar and hooked it to the tap. "Artie took care of his own," she said quietly.

"Wouldn't want you wasting away in this dive, if I know Artie." Earl's unfocused gaze swept the barroom, dark in the watery gray light of a California winter. A dozen mismatched wooden tables crowded into this front room, their equally mismatched chairs tucked neatly beneath them, the trails of their legs etched into the brown linoleum. Behind the bar and up a level, the Budweiser Clydesdales pranced in leaded glass formation above the pool table, throwing a blazing light on the green felt even as the corners of the room receded into murky shadow.

Meg lifted a case of Corona longnecks onto the cooler. This dialogue, repeated several times a week over the last five years, had long since become so scripted that she barely had to listen to hold up her end. Lately, she'd mostly given up responding at all. Earl knew her lines as well as she did, and if she missed her cue, he'd pause for about the right length of time and continue the conversation without her.

Not that there was all that much else to distract her on a rainy Tuesday afternoon. The last of the lunch crowd had left over an hour ago, and it would be another hour before her after-work regulars drifted in. Lupe was sweeping around the pool table in long, careful strokes, her waist-length black hair swaying to the rhythm of her broom. Old Nic sat slumped in his wheelchair at the table in the corner, nursing his coffee. He was looking thinner, Meg thought. She wondered if he still had the room on Edgeware, or if he was back on the street again.

"Lupe," she called.

The girl lifted her head. Meg motioned her over, ladled chili into a styrofoam bowl, and handed it to her carefully. "Take this to Mr. Nicholas."

Lupe took the bowl in both hands, dark eyes fixed on the contents as she maneuvered her way carefully between the empty tables. She set it down in front of old Nic with an air of triumph, then looked expectantly at Meg.

"Good girl, Lupe. Why don't you warm up Mr. Nic's coffee?"

Earl snorted again and pushed his shot glass toward her. "Fine lot you got in here," he muttered. "Bums and retards."

"Yeah, but you make up for all of 'em, Earl." Meg's voice went suddenly steely. She picked up Earl's glass and plunged it into the sink. "You gonna pay me for this, or you want it on your tab?"

Earl blinked. Her glare was steely, too, the navy blue eyes sparking with fury.

"Hell. I didn't mean nothin'," he said, digging in his

pocket for his money clip.

He was counting out singles when Julio Padilla burst through the front door, purple faced and bellowing in rapid-fire Spanish as he lurched toward Lupe. The girl was pouring coffee into old Nic's mug, so intent on the task that Julio was within arm's length before she saw him. She gasped and lurched backward. The pot flew out of her hand and crashed on the table in a shower of glass and hot liquid.

"*Puta!*" he shrieked, grabbing his daughter's arm with one hand as he drew the other back to strike her.

Earl was off his stool and across the room before the blow landed. In one quick motion, automatic after twenty-five years with the LAPD, he caught Julio's wrist, twisted it up between his shoulder blades, and shoved him down over the table.

"Easy, Julio," he said. "Don't make me break it."

"Papa!" Lupe cried.

Julio sneered at the girl as he writhed in the glass shards and steaming coffee. "*Puta!*" he repeated, and tried to spit. "You little whore!"

Earl jerked Julio upright, slammed him down much harder this time. "You watch your mouth, asshole. You want to call the cops, Meg?" He twisted the arm higher, and Julio yelped in pain. "I can just handle this here."

Meg was wiping her hands as she came around the bar, business-like, her round Irish face blank. "You have to leave, Julio," she said. "I told you, you can't come in here anymore."

Earl nodded and guided Julio to the front door. At the threshold, Earl gave him a shove that sent him hurtling out onto Sunset Boulevard. The little man stumbled, picked himself up, snarled something in Spanish, and scuttled toward the corner as a patrol car slowed in the street. Earl waved. The patrol car picked up speed and drove on.

Meg shut the door. "You didn't need to get that rough, Earl," she said.

"What was I supposed to do? I can't abide a man who hits women."

"Yeah, well, Lupe's gotta abide that bastard every day of her life. You take it a little too far, she pays." Meg pushed a stray salt-and-pepper ringlet into her chignon and stalked back toward the table where Lupe was winding Old Nic's hand in a yellow bandana.

"You hurt, Nic?" Meg asked.

"Fuck, it ain't nothin'," he growled, jerking his hand away from Lupe. "Can I get my goddamned coffee now?"

Lupe began clearing the glass and spilled coffee in nervous little swipes. Meg took the dishtowel from her.

"It's okay, honey," she said. "I got a fresh pot brewing. Why don't you get Mr. Nic a clean cup?"

"That bastard," Nic spat when Lupe was out of earshot. "Fuckin' bastard."

Meg shrugged. "Old story. I'll keep her with me until he cools off."

But Meg knew that now—particularly now—Lupe would not want to stay. Maybe, if she had lived up to her first bright promise, she would understand that her Papa was a man to be avoided in his tempers. But soon after her third birthday, Papa had shaken all of that promise out of his lively toddler, leaving her brain-injured and forever a child. Meg wondered if it really made any difference, if that lemming-en-route-to-the-ocean impulse wasn't more powerful than IQ. Lupe's mother had been bright enough. She'd worked for Artie back then, keeping the books. More than once, Meg and Artie offered her a place to go, money to leave, whatever she needed to get out. She had nonetheless stayed with her volatile husband until he beat her to death in a fit of rage. He got twenty years on a manslaughter conviction, and showed up at Meg's door in seven, demanding his fourteen-year-old daughter.

Lupe went with him willingly, her dark eyes adoring, so delighted to see her Papa after all this time. She remembered Papa's rages; she knew that he would beat her. Meg was quite sure of that. But he was her Papa, and like a docile little dog slinking back to a brutal master, Lupe followed him from hovel to hovel, willing to endure anything for his rare, treacherous expressions of affection. This time, Meg would insist that Lupe stay. She couldn't guess exactly what had triggered Julio's outburst, but Lupe had been more than a random target. To make matters worse, Julio had been thwarted in his fury by a fat *gringo* who tossed him out like old garbage. Home was not a safe place for Lupe this evening.

When the after-work crowd began to clear, Meg slipped through the small commercial kitchen to that portion of the original house that still served as her home. She went into Lupe's room, moved the stuffed bears off the bed, fluffed pillows, and turned back the pink chenille bedspread. In these last four years, Lupe still slept here when Papa disappeared for more than a day or two, or when his drunken rages drove his pretty, damaged daughter into the dark streets.

Meg dropped down on the bed. "This has to stop. One way or another, he's got to get out of that kid's life."

***

Earl was still sitting at the bar when she came downstairs. He'd stayed through the four-thirty crowd, drinking with the unlikely mix of lawyers and carpenters and musicians. Around six, as the last of the after-work regulars left for home and dinner, he switched to Diet Coke, sobering up for the drive back to his empty apartment.

"Chili?" Meg offered. "It's on the house. I'm gonna have Lupe clean out the pot in a minute."

Earl shook his head and pushed his fist into his diaphragm. "Damned heartburn. Where is that girl, anyway? I asked her for another Coke twenty minutes ago."

Meg stared at him. She dropped her ladle into the over-sized crock-pot, spun on her heel, and took the four steps to the back room in one bound.

"Lupe?"

Meg rattled the door marked "LADIES." It swung in on an empty toilet room.

Meg took a deep breath and made for the rear exit.

"Lupe?"

Security lights glared off the asphalt lot, empty but for Meg's rusty van and a single dumpster layered with graffiti.

Meg stalked back past the pool table, down the steps, and behind the bar.

"Outta here, you two," she said to Nic and Earl. She grabbed her jacket from its hook on the side of the back bar, checked the pocket for keys, and shoved a black cash bag into a plastic pickle bucket, snapping the lid shut as she went. "I'm closed."

"I'm coming with you," Earl said. He was already standing, sweater in hand, the bleary gray eyes suddenly very clear.

Old Nic maneuvered his chair back from the table

and began his painstaking roll toward the door. Meg came up behind him, grasped the handles of his chair, and pushed him out onto the wet sidewalk without breaking stride. She eyed the Sunset Boulevard traffic, gauging the headlights before she reached the curb.

Earl followed her as she dodged through four lanes of cars. He marveled at how quickly she moved. He thought of her as stocky—not fat, but square and short-legged, built for durability, not speed. He slammed his open palm against a blur of fender, dodged an oncoming motorcycle, and just caught a flash of her rounding the corner into a side street as he hit the sidewalk at a wheezing jog.

Two blocks up and a hundred plus years ago, some Victorian gentleman had built a three-story home into the side of the hill, well above the street. Beyond the wide granite stairs to the front porch, a shamble of chipped concrete steps led into what had once served as quarters for the hired help. In the decrepitude of the neighborhood, the house itself, and the finances of a more recent owner, servants' quarters had become a two-room apartment, rented to Julio Padilla in a moment of desperation and bad judgment.

Meg stood on the sidewalk, peering up at the fall of dark yard. As Earl reached her, she swore and lurched up the steps, veering into a tangle of weedy grass at the side of the building.

Earl followed. He didn't hear Lupe's small whimper until Meg dropped down beside her.

Meg's hand fluttered above the crumpled body, searching for contact with unwounded skin. Finally, she placed her open palm over the crown of Lupe's head. "I got you, honey. You're gonna be just fine," she said calmly, then to Earl, "Call..."

A car pulled into the curb half a block down. Lexus. Late model. Good bet, Earl decided. He lumbered toward it at a red-faced jog just as the driver heaved himself out.

"Hey, fella," Earl barked, pulling his wallet. "You got a cell phone?"

"Excuse me..." The driver edged back into his car.

"Police." Earl flashed his senior patrol badge. "Call 911. Got a girl hurt up there."

It couldn't have been more than ten minutes, but to Meg, the ambulance seemed to take forever. When it finally arrived, when they finally got Lupe inside, it careened through the streets in slow motion, the siren making an odd, under-water kind of whine through the pounding in her ears. She sat far back, out of the way of an attendant calling vital signs into a headset. She watched the color drain from Lupe's battered face, watched the bloodied lips pale, the one eye still visible behind the swelling go dull.

At the emergency room door, an exhausted resident took one look at the gray-faced girl on the gurney and burst into manic activity. Meg watched the staff flock around, then race the gurney down the hall and into an elevator. Sound muffled. Color muted. The air grew so heavy with the passing of seconds that she could barely breathe it. The elevator doors slid shut, and Meg slumped against the wall.

Later Earl found her in the waiting room and settled in beside her without a word. Afterwards, he would tell her how he'd roused Homicide Detective George Cicero at home. George didn't like the Padillas of the world, and he was nearly cheerful when Earl called in an old favor. Julio's parole officer would have a message when he walked in this morning, and with any luck, he'd be chatting with Julio in lock-up before lunch. If the girl died—

Earl looked at Meg, at the round Irish face, so perfectly composed, the square body perfectly still. Almost perfectly. He read the small tic just below her right eye, the odd whiteness around her lips. No. He wouldn't let himself think about that. For Meg's sake, Lupe couldn't die.

"I'm going to check with the desk again. You want coffee or something?" he asked.

Meg shook her head. "I gotta go home for a little while. My cleaners can take the deliveries, but I gotta get them a note."

Earl nodded. "I'll call you when she's out of surgery."

He walked with her as far as the nurse's station, then watched her until she was through the automatic doors, hailing a cab from the queue at the curb. He glanced at his watch. 2:00 AM. Lupe had gone into surgery a little after ten.

She came out at five, minus her spleen, her uterus, and both ovaries. The surgeon had pinned her pelvis together, and noted in the chart that she would require physical therapy. He also suggested referral to a gynecologist for hormone replacement, particularly as the surgery had terminated her pregnancy.

Meg returned to the hospital a little after 5:30, while Lupe was in the recovery room.

"That's why he's so pissed off," Earl said. "You think it was his?"

Meg shrugged. "Hell, she's so vulnerable. It could have been anybody."

Earl left her in conversation with the attending physician and went to call Cicero. He got a clerk with a thick accent he could neither peg nor understand, and hoped that her gargled response translated to, "I'll transfer you."

He held for longer than he thought he should, and was just about to hang up when Cicero's deep basso rumbled through the receiver.

"I didn't forget you, Earl. Got a guy headed your way for the report," Cicero told him. "Not a homicide yet, is it? Good. But while we're on the subject, you still hanging out at that place up on Sunset?"

"Ortiz's. Yeah."

"Steagal just took a call there. Cleaning crew found some guy in a dumpster."

"What guy?"

"Don't know. Give Steagal an hour, maybe he can tell you."

"Shit." Earl looked at his watch. Rush hour started early in L.A. The locals would already be rolling into Sunset on their way to work, probably slowing to gawk at the gathering of patrol cars and the coroner's wagon parked too prominently at Meg's front door. This couldn't be good for business.

Earl thanked Cicero and hung up. He checked his watch again. If he left now, he'd probably catch Steagal at the scene. He thought about telling Meg, decided against it. She had enough on her mind right now.

Shit. There, of all places. Last night, of all times. Neither of them had thought to lock the gates across the driveway when they raced out. And the lot was private in a way that few places along Sunset were, with the bar and house "L"-ing across the front and down one side, a steep rise of hillside obscuring the back, and the blank stucco wall of Rosa's Beauty Palace bounding it on the west. He pictured Meg paying the cabby, then fumbling with her keys on the dark street when she returned this morning. Had the dead man been lurking in the lot, waiting for her? Had whoever killed him been there, too?

Steagal was walking toward him down the driveway as Earl got out of the Buick. "Hey, Earl, is that you?" Steagal called. "Little early for a beer."

"No such thing as early. I'm retired." Then, quietly, as he and Steagal met at the curb, "Help me out here, Bob. Nice lady owns this joint. What's the story?"

Steagal shrugged. "Older couple cleans the place. The husband takes out the trash this morning and finds a guy dead in the dumpster. The coroner says the guy's neck is broken."

"How long?"

"Four to six, according to the tech."

"I.D.?"

"Male Hispanic, probably forties. Five-sixish, about 165. No papers." Both men turned at the squeak and clatter of a gurney wheeling toward them down the driveway. "Wanta have a look?"

Steagal motioned to the gurney operator, who stopped at the sidewalk and waited while Steagal unzipped the body bag to just below the corpse's chin.

Earl snorted. "Guess I should give Cicero a call. Save everybody a little paperwork." He glanced at Steagal, who stared back at him blankly. "I called him on a battery beef last night. Guy nearly killed his daughter." He pointed at the still body of Julio Padilla. "This guy."

Steagal pulled a notebook from his pocket and began to write. Earl knew the drill, rattling off answers in anticipation of Steagal's questions. Julio Padilla, vagrant, two-time loser. A hothead with enemies. Lots of 'em.

Earl drew a deep breath. "Guess I might as well tell you. The lady who owns this place—she's no fan."

Steagal shrugged, his expression decidedly skeptical. "That dumpster's pretty slimy. The dead guy wasn't gonna win any personal hygiene awards, but believe me, he wasn't moving when he went in. Not enough muck. Body isn't scuffed up either. Looks like somebody picked him up and heaved him right over the side. You think she could do that?"

"No." Earl shook his head. "No, not even pissed. Hell, she's in her mid-forties, maybe Padilla's height and a little dumpy."

"Think she could snap his neck?"

"I think she'd like to, but no, not really."

"She got any helpful friends?"

"Not for that kind of project."

"Okay, then how about the guy? He carry any money? Drugs, maybe?"

"Not likely. He was more of a Thunderbird kinda guy."

"Real piece of shit, huh?"

"Five-star."

Steagal flipped his notebook shut and thanked Earl for coming down. Earl watched as he spoke briefly to a bored-looking evidence technician, then gave the high sign to an equally disinterested coroner's assistant. The van pulled into traffic and drove off at a little less than the speed limit. Nobody was going to be missing any coffee breaks over this one.

On his way back to the hospital, Earl stopped at 7-Eleven and picked up one of everything greasy and loaded with sugar. Meg must be running on adrenaline by now. Assuming that Lupe was stable, he'd drive her down to the division this afternoon, let Steagal get her statement, then take her home to get some sleep.

Meg was pacing the hall outside of intensive care, waiting for the next ten-minute period when hospital rules allowed her into Lupe's room. He hugged her awkwardly.

"She's hanging in there." Meg's voice had gone flat. "They gave her a lot of blood, but the doctor says she's gonna make it."

"Hey, that's great. Let's sit in here for a minute," Earl said, steering her toward the waiting room. "You heard me talk about Cicero? Guy I used to partner with? I woke him up last night, asked him to get the ball rolling on this one."

Meg dropped into a thinly upholstered chair. "Oh. They're going after Julio then."

"Yes."

"They won't do anything. They never do."

"Doesn't matter." He peeled the coffee lid back and handed her the cup. "They found him this morning, Meg. He's dead."

Meg stared at him for maybe ten seconds before she spoke. "Dead? You're sure?"

"I saw him. He was stiffening up pretty good."

She set the paper cup down very, very carefully, then stood and headed for the door.

"Where are you going?" he asked.

"To call an attorney."

Earl felt a tightening in his throat. Why would Meg think she needed an attorney? He hadn't said how Padilla died, or even where he was found. *Looks like somebody picked him up and heaved him right over the side.* He cocked his head, assessing the square body. Could she —?

"Lupe's going to need a guardian," Meg said.

* * *

It was Monday, the only day that Ortiz's didn't open for business. A hot October Monday. The house and bar were shut up tight, the air conditioner humming at full power, as Meg walked through the rooms, touching the smooth, cool wood of the bar, the steel countertops in the kitchen, the back of Artie's old recliner. She had lived twenty years in these rooms. Good years, all of them.

Julio Padilla had been dead for eight months. The police had no suspects, but Earl assured her that they would eventually clear the case. Some street punk would turn up with Julio's green card in his wallet, or get stopped on Julio's driver's license. Meg nodded and said nothing.

Last week, she had sent Lupe to St. Louis to stay with Meg's sister while Meg got the place ready to sell. Lupe had called her this morning, a little apprehensive, still a little worn, but generally cheerful, bubbling over about her visit to the zoo. Aunt Sandy was nice to her. When would Meg be coming?

Soon now.

The broker would be here tomorrow morning at ten. Meg had a few more small repairs, a few more things to pack away before she let the rest of the world in.

The back door, for example. She examined the crack in the wooden panel.

Julio had been on a tear when he did that. Drunk. Pounding on the door and screaming in Spanish for Lupe to come out. He hadn't finished with her, the little whore, the little *puta.*

Meg had only just come back from the hospital, and was in the kitchen writing instructions for Mrs. Aguilar. For a moment she'd stood rigid, rage bleeding through her, so huge that the weight of it nearly suffocated her. She'd heard the crack of the wood, and the rage ran cold as ice water, surreally calm.

Meg went to the broom closet, searched among the jars and cans that clutter the top shelf, pulled down a small plastic container of wood filler. This would work, she decided, and rummaged for a putty knife and sandpaper. She'd fill the crack and give the door a coat of paint.

She sat down at the small metal table to begin her list. Paint. Blue for the door. She leaned back in her chair to survey the kitchen. Perhaps she should move some things out to make the room look bigger. There really wasn't space for this table and chairs.

That evening, when she had finally persuaded Julio that Lupe wasn't here, that he should come sit down so they could think together where she might have gone, Meg had felt how close the space was. When she got up to walk around him, she'd turned a little sideways, brushed against him in passing. That was when he had made the sound, that deep in his chest, purring noise, like a tomcat in rut, and leaned his greasy black head into her breast. She had stopped still, listening to the rush of blood in her ears, feeling that deadly calm bloom into purpose.

"You poor man," she'd crooned, drawing her hand across his chest, his throat, along his jaw. "You poor, poor man."

He had turned halfway in his chair—this very chair—far enough for her to see the leering grin, the drunken glitter of his eye. He would have Arturo Ortiz's *gringa* tonight, his fine Irish woman. He would—

Her face—it must have been something in her face. In the last instant, Julio's leer had turned to horror, and she felt him stiffen in her grip. Too late. Her left hand braced against his ear, and she snapped his head toward her with a muffled pop.

Meg rose and went into her bedroom. She smoothed the comforter with one rough hand, plumped the pillows. The family pictures would stay, of course. The broker had told her that family pictures lent warmth. Artie with Candy, their golden retriever. Meg and Artie in front of the Gateway Arch, Sandy's daughter riding on Artie's shoulders. Meg and Sandy as young teens, clowning on a carousel horse.

She would dig out more like these, or paint the wall when she took down the others. She ran her index finger along the frame of her favorite—her championship lift in the summer of '82, the sun gleaming off her bulging shoulders as she held two hundred and sixty pounds against her chest. She would crate the two-dozen trophies and send them ahead. She held up the gleaming brass torso of a muscular woman curling a dumb bell into her body. She smiled to herself, reading the inscription. "Meg O'Daniel, Women's All Around, Venice Beach, 1986." Maybe one day when she was very, very old, she would send this one back to Earl. She suspected he'd understand.

She went to get a box and newspaper from the storage closet. As she entered the kitchen, she paused, gauging the room again.

Yes, she decided, it would show much better without the furniture. She would have Mr. Aguilar put the table in the dumpster tomorrow. She would keep the chairs.

At least, she would keep one of them.

The journey down Sunset Boulevard officially starts at Beaudry Avenue, an invisible line of demarcation at which point the street changes from Cesar E. Chávez Avenue, the recently renamed thoroughfare that courses up from East Los Angeles. This once oil-rich stretch of the boulevard is now dotted with vacant lots and the ruins of former buildings, strange indicators of an area that for decades has appeared to rebuff attempts at rehabilitation (and surprising sights for those who accept the canard that Los Angeles is a city with no history). The shadows of the downtown skyscrapers do not reach here, and no one can count the number of lives that have similarly fallen out of reach...

BEAUDRY ROSE

By Gayle McGary

He was waiting for me at the southeast intersection of Sunset and Beaudry. He was easy to spot—an older white guy, tall and skinny, in a dusty brown suit and hat. On a hot Saturday afternoon in downtown L. A. he was a fish out of water; a suit stuck in a rushing river of neighborhood residents in their Southern California attire that parted right and left of him and flowed on.

I turned onto Beaudry and then swung into a fast-food parking lot. I got out and jogged up to Sunset to meet him.

"Mr. Hanson?"

"Yes?" He looked startled to hear his name spoken even though we had talked on the phone and had set up this meeting the day before.

"I'm Kim Rush, your nephew Manny's teacher." I stuck out my hand, and he put down a small black suitcase to take it. His hand was bony, cold, and dry, but his grip was firm.

"Manny?" he asked, looking momentarily confused. Then the light came on. "Forgive me, but my sister's grandson has always been Emanuel to me. I am Matthew Hanson." He nodded at the end of each sentence as though to emphasize his words.

"Let's get out of the sun. Why don't we have something down at the restaurant?" I pointed toward the fast food place.

"Fine, fine." Hanson mopped his brow with a yellowed handkerchief.

We both ordered coffee and sat at a table near the window. Hanson set his suitcase on the floor and laid his brown hat on the table beside his cup. Perspiration had glued his silver-white hair to his head.

"Now, I want to tell you right off that I am grateful you have agreed to help me."

His voice was deep and sonorous. I knew from Manny that his granduncle was a preacher, the leader of an evangelical congregation back in his hometown in Wisconsin. Manny always referred to him as "the Preacher, a real serious Jesus jumper who thinks everything is a sin." Now, hearing his voice, I could well imagine it reaching out to reel in his flock and ready them to hit the road to salvation.

"You're welcome," I said. "I'll help if I can." An awkward silence fell between us, and for a few moments we both sipped our coffees and stared out the window. I concentrated on deciphering the elaborate graffiti covering the cinder block wall across the street and wondered what the hell I thought I was doing here. Helping Manny, I hoped. Manny was my student in painting at Angels Arts Loft, a community outreach center for at-risk kids.

I tried some more small talk. "Is this your first trip to Los Angeles?"

"It is." His eyes were a piercing blue with a fiery glint. "I'm staying over there at the Paradise Motel." He pointed out the window at an old L-shaped motel half-hidden behind a new single story neighborhood medical clinic. The graffiti had spread from the wall to the motel units. There were two cars parked by the clinic and none at the motel.

"There's a brand new Holiday Inn up Sunset a few blocks," I said.

"The Paradise will do fine." It was clear from his tone that he felt I'd criticized his choice.

"Oh, I saw the suitcase and I thought..." I quickly changed the subject. "Manny...I mean, Emanuel asked me to help you find an artist—your brother, is it?"

"I want some pictures he has. I will pay you."

"I wouldn't accept payment, Mr. Hanson." I didn't want the favor I'd agreed to do for my student to turn into a contract for hire. I didn't want an obligation that I wasn't at all sure I could fulfill.

"I'm not a detective," I continued. "I'm an artist. I work with troubled kids and— "

"I know all about what you do with drugged children," he said, cutting me off. "And I do not want a detective. I have no interest in associating with a godless mercenary of the law."

Hanson's voice had risen, and out of the corner of my eye I saw faces turn in our direction. Then he became aware of people's stares and spoke more quietly. "Forgive me. My wife recently passed away and I am still grieving. I will be in your debt if you can find the pictures. They're of my daughter."

"I'm sorry for your loss," I said, making a mental note not to get the guy riled up. "I'll help any way I can."

Hanson said nothing. He bent to open his suitcase and pulled out a small roll of canvases.

The paintings were small—none larger than twenty by thirty inches. The one on top was a portrait of a little girl seated primly in a straight-backed chair, her legs crossed at the ankles with her feet in polished black

Maryjane shoes. She wore a white dress with pink ribbons, and there were pink ribbons in her blond hair. Her hands, folded in her lap, held a white rose. She stared straight out at the viewer, a solemn expression on her face, a proper little five-or-six-year-old.

"She's beautiful," I said.

Hanson said nothing. He rolled up the painting and put it to one side to reveal another painting of the girl, at a later age, nine or ten. In this one she held a New Testament as well as a rose.

"Manny told me her name is Rose," I said, uncomfortable with Hanson's silence. "It's a lovely name."

"'The wilderness and the solitary place shall be glad for them; and the desert shall rejoice and blossom as the rose,'" he intoned, as he unrolled another painting of his daughter.

There were four paintings in all. The artist was clearly self-taught, struggling with awkward proportions and faulty perspective. But as the girl matured, so did the artist's talent. Rose's body filled out into that of a young woman's, and her expression brightened as though she had found more joy in each passing year.

In the fourth painting, which, Hanson informed me, had been painted when his daughter was twelve years old, the painter was handling form and color with more authority. His grasp of perspective had improved. The young girl was standing, the contours of her body modeled with an intense physicality, while her face was bathed in a clear golden light. It was clear the artist was celebrating her budding womanhood. Innocence and eroticism. A voluptuous angel.

The rose motif continued, but now as a bouquet, the

colors a wild array of reds, pinks and corals. It was embarrassingly easy to read the symbology of sexual awakening. I wondered if Hanson was aware of it.

"My brother Thomas and I took different paths," Hanson said. "When he left our town five years ago, he changed his name. Our family's name was not good enough for the great artist. I don't know what he calls himself now, but I have good reason to believe he lives in Los Angeles. I want you to find him so that I may get the other pictures of Rose—the ones he took with him." Hanson began to lay the paintings one on top of the other, smoothing them out until they could be rolled together.

"Your brother has a style that is often referred to as 'naïf' or 'visionary,'" I said. "It usually means that the artist is self-taught. Do you know if he went on to study art at a school?"

"No, I do not. I am not interested in my brother. My only interest is in the pictures of my daughter."

"I'll need to take the paintings with me to show around to some people," I said. "To see if anyone recognizes his style. It's the only way I could hope to find him."

"These are my most precious possessions. I entrust them to you because I must." His eyes were hard as though to emphasize the degree of accountability to which I would be held if I betrayed his trust. I looked away.

Part of me wanted to tell the old cuss where to stuff his precious possessions. I knew he was pestering Manny's grandmother because he believed she knew where their brother Thomas was. This worried me because anything that bothered Manny's grandmother bothered Manny. He was a kid living on the edge, and it wouldn't take much to push him over. I wanted to get rid of the Preacher, but it looked like I'd have to find his brother and the paintings of his daughter to do that. I didn't like the guy, but the truth was, I felt a little sorry for him.

"Okay," I said, "I'll try. But I'm not too optimistic about finding your brother. Los Angeles is a big place. He may not be in this area." I picked up the rolled canvases and tucked them under my arm. Hanson's eyes followed them. "I'll take good care of these."

I stood to leave, feeling a lot less charitable than I had an hour before. I seemed to have picked up Hanson's gloom. He retrieved his suitcase from the floor and we walked outside into the late afternoon sun.

I could have asked Matthew Hanson why he was so bent on getting some of his brother's paintings that he traveled two thousand miles to hand over his most precious possessions to a stranger and ask for her help. But I knew the answer. Manny had already told me that his Aunt Rose was dead and that the Preacher was crazy on the subject. Manny thought the Preacher wanted the pictures because he was planning to build a shrine to his dead daughter.

"Emanuel has a good eye," I said, trying to end the meeting on a positive note. "Has he shown you any of his drawings?"

"My sister is soft on the boy. He should be made to get a paying job. I don't doubt that his idea of art is that defacement of property over there." He nodded his head toward the graffiti on the wall across the street.

We were standing on Beaudry, facing west. In front of us, between the graffitied wall and the Paradise Motel, was a vacant lot filled with broken concrete, twisted steel and weeds. To our left and higher on the horizon, rush hour traffic clogged the Hollywood Freeway. The downtown skyline appeared so close as to be in throwing distance.

"Rose lived on this street," Hanson said.

I looked at him in surprise. There were very few residential structures left on Beaudry, and none at all in the direction Hanson was looking. They had all been razed, including a small neighborhood church, to make way for the Belmont Learning Complex, a project now on semi-permanent hold while the political powers figured out what to do about the toxic fumes and methane gas that poisoned the ground below. I wondered how Rose had died, and where. Out here in Los Angeles? On this street? Was Hanson visiting the terrible place where she had met her death?

"I am in your debt," Hanson said. "I trust you are a God-fearing woman, Miss Rush."

"No, not really," I said hesitantly, hoping I wouldn't bring on any devil lectures. "Goodbye, Mr. Hanson. I'll call you. If I can help you at all, I should know something in a couple of days."

"Thank you," he said without looking at me, and crossed the street.

I watched him walk across the Paradise Motel parking lot and set down his suitcase in front of a unit with a big blue twelve painted on the door. It was the unit nearest the trash-filled vacant lot, and I wondered if he had chosen it simply to be able to look out on Beaudry and remember his dead daughter.

Then I really did feel sorry for the guy. His wife had just died, and that had freed him to come out here to visit a poisoned vacant lot where his daughter had lived and may have died. He might be building a shrine to her, and he had a snowball's chance in hell of finding those pictures of his daughter.

Hanson unlocked the door of number twelve, picked up his suitcase, went inside and closed the door. I wondered why he kept the suitcase so close to him, why he even carried it with him. He didn't need it to hold the small roll of canvases I now had under my arm. I figured the Preacher probably worried about godless burglars. Or, maybe it was a portable shrine.

* * *

"So, you don't have enough to do helping messed-up juvies, you've got to take on their messed-up grandpas." Rick was fixing me a tall iced cappuccino behind the counter of his café gallery. He set it down in front of me and leaned his tattooed arms on the counter. His spiked hair was blue this week. He wore three small gold hoops in his left ear. He was my best friend.

Rick looked at the canvases we had rolled out and held open with sugar and cinnamon shakers on their corners. "And what's with this crap? Why would anybody go looking for more of it?"

"First off, it's Manny's granduncle I'm helping, not his grandpa," I said. "The paintings are of the guy's dead daughter, and he wants more of them. If there *are* more, that is. And if I can find them. Anyway, I think they're kind of interesting. Sort of 'art brut.' Kind of raw. After meeting the Preacher, I'm wondering how weird his brother is."

"Yeah, I think the guy's probably as raw as his paintings, and I think he's got a thing for little girls." Rick looked at me. "I see you do, too. Why do you want to waste your time looking for some bad paintings by some badass who may be dead, for all you know? And this

Preacher guy sounds like a real turd."

"Because Manny's in a bad place right now and I promised him I would help."

"Manny's still coming to the Loft, isn't he?"

"Yes, but something's up with him. He could go back to using and be in deep shit before I knew what was happening. I don't know if I could get him out of it this time." I became aware of my hands gripping my cold glass of coffee. My voice was tight. "But I do know that having the Preacher leaning on him and spouting fire and brimstone is going to make things even worse."

"Hey, I like the kid. But you can't save everybody." Rick knew what he was talking about. He'd been a social worker for ten years until he decided that making people a good cup of coffee was something he could do whereas making people's lives better was an impossible dream. "Some people just have a shitload of grief, and you can't lighten their load."

"Just give me your thoughts on these, okay? Let's say Brother Badass gets better as a painter. Who might be showing his work if he was still in L. A.?" Rick managed to keep up with the art culture in Los Angeles better than I did. He mounted small exhibitions for emerging artists, and artists at all stages of their careers hung out at his café.

"You're hoping he's stayed figurative and stuck to this rose theme or gone on to some other flower-cum-sex symbols. No pun intended. Har, har."

"No pun accepted," I said. "This last painting..." I pointed to the one of Rose at twelve, standing at an open window. She was in profile, gazing out, with sunlight streaming in like the hand of God, illuminating the bounty of roses in her arms. "It's dated only five years ago, and the guy had been stuck on the rose thing for seven years already. It's an obsession. He's probably not given it up completely. It's so obvious, and the strange thing is that the Preacher doesn't seem to have caught on to the symbolism."

"People see what they want to see. They know what they want to know." Rick rolled up the paintings. "Okay, I'll see what I can find out. I'll talk it around. Maybe the dude comes in here all the time, and all I have to do is ask who paints roses on little girls. Got an idea. Whyn'tcha leave the paintings here. I'll hang a couple, maybe sombody'll recognize them."

* * *

The Loft, as everybody familiar with Angels Arts Loft refers to it, is not far from Rick's place. It's just a little further down Sunset toward downtown, where the Silver Lake district turns into Echo Park, on the second floor of an old warehouse. The bottom floor houses a small Salvadoran market and a hair salon. I had a painting class at five o'clock, and I was expecting Manny.

By five-thirty there was no sign of Manny, which was unusual. We don't pry into the kids' lives; they don't have enough privacy as it is—living as they do in foster homes, juvenile hall, and sometimes even on the street. And we try not to check up on them, so they feel we trust them. But I was worried, so I called his grandmother.

"We haven't met, Mrs. Cleveland," I said. "I'm Kim Rush, Manny's teacher at Angels Arts Loft."

"Oh, yes, Manny speaks of you often. What can I do for you?"

"Manny was supposed to be here for class at five o'clock. He didn't show up. Did anything happen?"

She was silent.

"Mrs. Cleveland, has something happened to him?"

"Manny got into a fight with his uncle. He just ran right out of here."

"Is Mr. Hanson still there?"

"No. He left, too. He was very angry. He doesn't believe me that I don't know where our brother Thomas is. I don't know what to do."

"I'm sure everything will be fine," I said, not sure if I believed myself. I was scared for Manny. He had been on some kind of drugs for most of his thirteen years. His grandmother had raised him from a toddler, apparently. I didn't know where his mother was or even if she was alive. There was no father in the picture. Granduncle Matthew sure wasn't the one to fit the bill right now. I told Mrs. Cleveland I would call her if Manny showed up at the Loft. Then I called Rick.

"Bingo, babe," he said. "Talk about beginner's luck! This is unreal! Couple of guys from that big downtown art co-op were in—you know, the place that has open studios? One of them thought he recognized your weirdo artist. Couldn't remember his name, but he told me which studio he's at. Seems like he's still doing paintings of girls with flowers, only now they aren't dressed so pretty. In fact, they aren't dressed at all."

"How old are they?"

"The guys from the co-op?"

"The women in the paintings, Rick."

"Oh, he didn't say. But he mentioned that the guy is also into photography now. Same thing: photos of girls and flowers. Anyway, there isn't a hundred percent guarantee that this is your painter, but from what I know of the co-op dude, he's got an eye for personal style that even museums trust. I'd put money down that it's your guy. And, hey, if you want company when you go looking for him, I'm free. Two of my workers just came in."

"I think I'd better visit the Preacher first and see if I can rein him in. He was at Manny's grandmother's a short while ago. There was some kind of fight, and Manny hasn't shown up here yet. Can you meet me over at Sunset and Beaudry with the paintings? The Preacher is staying at the Paradise Motel."

"Where else? Okay, you got it."

Things were moving fast. Worried as I was about Manny, it looked like we would be free of the Preacher soon.

I called Matthew Hanson at the Paradise Motel and told him I might have some news for him. He told me he was just about to go out and asked me if I would look for him down Beaudry near First.

* * *

It was dark when Rick and I met in the motel parking lot, and we drove down Beaudry toward First Street in my car. It was a grim area. With the houses gone, street people had erected shelters of their own out of cardboard boxes and packing cases. Under the freeway a group was huddled around a fire they had going in a trash can. It wasn't very cold, but I knew that people who had lived a long time on the streets could never get warm enough.

We found the Preacher on the sidewalk, staring through a chain link fence topped with razor wire and hung with "No Trespassing" signs. On the other side was dirt and grass and chunks of concrete illuminated by security lights, and a ways down and back up the hill, the unfinished Belmont Learning Complex. Hanson didn't turn to look at us as we came up beside him.

"Rose bushes grew here," he said. "Rose told me she planted them. Now they say the land is poisoned."

"You don't know the half of it, Rev," Rick said.

I pinched his arm.

"What?"

"Quiet," I said. I stepped closer to the Preacher. "Mr. Hanson, I'd like you to meet my friend, Rick. He's been helping me look for your brother." But the Preacher didn't appear to be listening.

"'There are serpents in the belly. How can ye escape the damnation of hell?'" the Preacher said.

"Mr. Hanson," I tried again. "We think we found your brother."

"'Charm is deceitful, and beauty is vain, but a woman who fears the Lord is to be praised.'" The Preacher's voice was spooky, ringing across the abandoned landscape.

"Mr. Hanson, we can go over there right now. I've brought back the paintings of Rose."

Hanson stooped to pick up his suitcase and followed us to the car. I couldn't imagine what he carried around in that thing. He got into the passenger seat. I gave him the paintings, and he stowed them away in his suitcase.

We headed south and east past the heart of downtown and into a district of big old buildings where yuppie businesses rubbed shoulders with storage warehouses and carton manufacturers.

I had visited the Art Co-op before, but didn't go often because the place was half full of artists and half full of people who were basically expensive boutique owners.

The "art" they exhibited tended toward feather jewelry, decorative fossils, and coffee table sculptures made out of crystals and driftwood. It seemed like the perfect place for a guy whose total body of work was a one-liner. I hoped we'd find the Preacher's brother here, and he could get the pictures of Rose that he wanted. And we could get rid of him.

Rick led us through a maze of small buildings to a six story one. We followed him into a freight elevator, and he hit a button for the third floor. We rode up in silence. Once out of the elevator, we followed Rick down the hall to an open door where he poked his head in and out, then pointed us further down the hall, until we came to a door with a stained glass window set into it. A rose, I was happy to see. I remembered that stained glass decorations were another art product people hawked down here. The sound of music came from inside. Rick knocked.

"'And the Lord has lifted the scales from mine eyes,'" the Preacher suddenly shouted, and I nearly jumped out of my skin. I was praying that this was the home of brother Thomas just so I didn't have to accompany the crazed old man anywhere else.

The door was opened by a man who looked a lot like the Preacher, only happy. He wore jeans and a paint-smeared muscle shirt. His graying hair was long and tied back in a ponytail, and he looked pretty buff. He also looked surprised as hell.

"Brother Thomas," said the Preacher, suddenly sounding normal. Brother Thomas just stared and said nothing.

Rick was pulling my arm, clearly wanting to leave, but I felt responsible for the old guy. Brother Thomas looked like he was capable of beating the crap out of his older brother.

"Will you be all right here, Mr. Hanson?" I asked.

"Go along now, children," Hanson said, stepping forward and never taking his eyes off his brother.

* * *

"Whew," I said when we got back down to the car. "I feel like I've just been in a movie. Did you see what I saw?"

"Where did you get these guys?" Rick said as he slid into the passenger seat. "Whoa. Wait. Guy left his suitcase."

"Goddamnit!" I said, slapping my hands on the steering wheel. "Do we really have to go back and give it to him?"

We looked at each other for a beat.

"I'll take it up," Rick said.

"I'll go with you," I said, sighing. "He's my guy. I'll see it through to the end. Maybe we'll find them laughing together over old times. Maybe looking for pictures of Rose was just an excuse for Hanson to patch things up with his brother. His wife just died. His daughter's dead. His grandnephew is a sinner. He doesn't have much family left."

We were just getting out of the elevator when we heard the shots. Then the screaming. The hall was instantly full of people. We started down the hall toward Thomas Hanson's studio, pushed from behind by the crowd. Voices asking: "What happened? Were those gunshots? Who is it? Who's screaming?"

Thomas Hanson's door was open. In the doorway stood a woman, her face in her hands, her screams reduced to rhythmic moans as she swayed from side to side.

"Somebody call 911!" I yelled. A couple of voices answered that they already had.

I went to the woman. "Are you all right?" I asked. "What happened?"

Over her shoulder I could see into the room. Overhead track lights illuminated photographs and paintings on the wall and the two bodies lying on the floor, one on top of the other. Blood seemed to be everywhere.

"It's all right," I said to the woman. "It's going to be all right."

"Jesus," Rick muttered, dropping the suitcase. It sprang open on impact with the floor, spilling out all its contents.

The woman took her hands away from her face and looked at me.

"He shot him," she cried, her voice a wail, her head whipping from side to side. "And then, he shot himself." Her eyes were wide, staring into mine. "He didn't shoot me because he said I was already...already..."

"Jesus, is that Rose?" Rick said from behind me. "I thought you said she was dead."

I turned toward him and, for the first time, saw the contents of the Preacher's suitcase: photos—fashion shots and light cheesecake—and videotapes, soft porn by the look of them.

"Maybe she *was* to him," I said.

I held Rose until the police and the ambulance came.

A drive through the Echo Park district of Los Angeles is like a trip into the past. Streets lined with ornate Victorian homes meet others with vintage Spanish architecture, some of which has gone unaltered since the 1920s. Lotus-covered Echo Park Lake, just a stone's throw from Sunset, continues to be used as a location for period films, with virtually no alteration needed to recreate a moment of long-ago Los Angeles. One almost expects to see a clanging Pacific Electric Red Car, another ghost of Los Angeles that was the city's primary mode of transportation for much of the first half of the twentieth century.

In fact, isn't that one right there, just up ahead?

THE RED CAR MURDERS

by Richard Partlow

It's 1946 in Los Angeles and I'm just a kid. The war's over and I live alone with my dad who isn't home much, since he's out looking for work. I sell newspapers to help out. Two months ago, after Dad got back from the war, my mom hopped a streetcar for her family get-together in Iowa. A few days later she sent us a postcard saying she was staying awhile. It would be nice to have someone at home, waiting for me.

I'm in the seventh grade at Thomas Starr King Junior High. I live in Echo Park, have a BB gun, and sell papers working the white line dividing the traffic lanes on San Pedro at First in Japantown. After school I ride the big Pacific Electric Red Cars that rumble and clang along Sunset. I rode them even during the Red Car Murders.

Today the big Red Car with orange and silver electric wings painted on its front ground to a stop at Fountain. It was a cold wintry day, and I climbed through the side rear window for my usual free ride, enjoying the hot smell of the electric motors and worn metal. I ignored the passengers in the back of the Red Car. I was a blur, just a kid.

I quickly lifted the long seat under the window where the motorman stores stuff and grabbed inside for my dynamite caps—really torpedoes, but I like to say dynamite caps. They are big as a quarter and are used to stop the Red Cars in emergencies. I'd put them on Red Car tracks along with pennies that needed squashing and then watch from the curb as the 500-pound wheels roll over them. The dynamite caps make a great noise, like exploding big old bombs. The motormen were supposed to stop the Red Car when they heard them. Danger ahead. They never did stop. I guess they figured it was kid games. Even when I hid in the tall grass and they couldn't see me. How did they know?

My hand touched cold metal and I peeked under the seat. It was a small silver gun. I grabbed it, stole a few dynamite caps, and stuffed them all in my jacket pocket. I sat on the seat looking innocent and feeling smartass, like Pat Novak in my favorite radio mystery, *Pat Novak For Hire*. He walked around at night solving mysteries in the San Francisco fog. I checked out the Red Car, hoping I looked like Pat—tough, sizing up the situation. It's hard to think of smartass remarks.

There were a few people in the back seats. The guy across the aisle from me had a big black beard and dirty black clothes and was shelling peanuts. Blackbeard the Peanut Eater. The Red Car picked up speed, sending passengers lurching up the aisle like Lon Chaney, Jr. in his mummy movies, and grabbing at the silver handles on the seats. The motorman up front was busy taking transfers, making change, clanking his bell at cars, spitting out the window.

I pressed my pocket against me, wondering why a gun was under the motorman's storage seat. Jesus Happy Christ! I had the Red Car killer's gun in my pocket! The newspapers said he shot gangsters. A motorman found one, shot dead at the end of the Red Car shortline in Echo

Park near my house. Another gangster was shot by the tracks, in the dark. Wrote in his own blood, but died and messed up the words. The last one died in back of a Red Car, where I was. I wondered why so many gangsters were kicking the bucket. What would Pat Novak do? I stared hard at the floor, my mouth dry. I figured the killer was on board, watching over his hidden gun, so he saw me steal it. He was probably planning to kill me with his gun that was in my pocket. Could I put it back?

Pat Novak in my mind, in his flat voice, said, "Too late, dummy, look around you." Blackbeard was glaring at me and dropping peanut shells all over the place. He looked nutso and was mumbling like he hated me, shoving peanuts in his mouth, broken peanuts dribbling down his black beard. A pirate with crazy blue eyes fixed on my forehead. Nutso enough to kill.

People in the back looked at me, curious like. The man in a brown vested suit leaning against a back window raised an eyebrow in my direction and looked out the window. Was he signaling me? The woman with red hair in the seat to my right was looking in a little round mirror, doing her lips, cyes crossed. Staring at me? I narrowed my eyes to make myself small and swore I'd never steal dynamite caps again. Not till this blew over.

Finally, I just couldn't take all that attention and got off long before my stop. I hiked a good forty-five minutes, stopping for traffic signals so no cop would nail me and find a gun on me. I buttoned my jacket all the way up because a cold January wind was following me. I was late for work, but I looked around to see if I was being followed. Just tons of people in a hurry, like the shadows of the clouds were chasing them.

At my corner at First and San Pedro, I untied my papers, flapping in the wind, put a broken brick on top, tied on my dark green change apron, and grabbed some bulldog and sunset editions of the pink *Daily News* and green *Herald Express*. I scanned them. They thought the killer might be a rogue cop, getting even on his own.

I worked the going-home traffic, some cars with headlights already on. I hurried along the white line between the two lanes, dodging cars and big rigs, holding up headlines, folding papers into an upside down V so I could hand them through windows with one hand, palm up and cupped to receive the money. My other hand was free to make change, pick my nose, flip a finger at anybody who drove too close to my feet.

Once, I thought I saw Nutso on the corner stuffing peanuts in his mouth, his eyes on me. I froze, but he slipped behind the people waiting to cross the street. Was it him? Pat Novak would have walked over and made sure. I also saw a red-haired woman, and a guy in a brown vested suit. So what? I'd really get tricked if I saw the Red Car motorman walking toward me, his hand out, demanding his fare.

In the curb lane, four cars up, I recognized the 1937 gray Plymouth coupe with Officer Dotty Sullivan behind the windshield in her police uniform. My favorite customer. I ran past the cars to her and handed her a *Daily News*. She plunked the money in my palm. She knows me and we talk a lot, even when the light turns green.

"Thanks, Dotty." I glanced at the green light and back at her face. She gave me her Katharine Hepburn look, like it was just me and her in an empty street. Behind her, the man in the square black 1926 Nash with window shades tooted his horn. Goose farts. The trucker in the blue rig behind the Nash leaned on his air horn and blasted. I covered my ears. The Nash motor quit and the guy ground his starter and tapped out more goose farts. They'd be there awhile.

"Can I talk to you?" I shouted to Dotty.

Dotty's dark green eyes stared at me, and she pointed around the corner. I followed her as she made her turn and parked in the red at the curb. Cars were honking at her to get out of the way. She turned on a red searchlight on the driver's side and aimed it at the traffic behind her. The horns stopped.

"Mark, what is it?" she said, sounding like she cared.

I leaned through her passenger window, feeling better already, not sure what to say. The gun in my pocket banged on her door. I pulled my pocket back. A killer was looking for me, but I was too chicken to give her the gun. I didn't want her to know I'd stolen the gun and the dynamite caps and hadn't paid the fare. I wanted her to still like me.

"Oh, I just wanted to say hi," I said.

"Hi." She brushed her brown hair back from her ear.

"I rode the Red Car today, but I got off early and walked to work," I said.

"Say, why walk in this weather? It's cold and it's going to rain." She leaned toward the passenger window and put her finger on my nose. "Did you climb in through the window again and the motorman caught you and threw you off?" She laughed.

"Yes, and no, he didn't throw me off," I said.

"Did somebody touch you on the streetcar?" she said. "Like we talked about?"

I shook my head.

"Well, what are you telling me?"

"I saw a scary nutso guy on the Red Car and maybe again here on the corner."

"You think he's following you?" she said.

"Maybe."

"What's he look like?"

"The Red Car killer. He's got a big black beard, like Blackbeard the Pirate, messy old black clothes, eats peanuts, talks to himself, and he doesn't like me."

She shook her head. "Sounds like he's just a nut on his own planet. Mark, I'm glad you talked to me. Listen, it's smart to be careful. Use the eyes in the back of your head. Don't hang around after work. Go home to your dad. How's he doing?"

"Still looking for work," I said. "Stays out a lot."

"Hear from your mom?"

"They talk on the phone. She's not ready to come back."

Her lips got tight. "Lot of G.I.'s coming back are looking for work. It's hard for everyone. Okay, from now on, you pay the motorman, Mark. He's gotta eat too, you know. Ride up front where he can plainly see you. Hear me? You're just a kid. Take care."

She smiled. She trusted me. If she found out I stole a gun and dynamite caps, she'd have to arrest me. I changed the subject.

"I didn't know you had a red searchlight," I said.

"I bought it." She put a keep-a-secret finger to her lips. "I'm not supposed to have a red light, or a gun. I'm just a woman." She winked at me. "Sound familiar, kid?"

She drove off, her engine coughing, puffing black clouds out of the tailpipe. Everybody kept their old cars because they stopped making new ones during the war. Kept them together with cardboard gaskets, wood chips in the oil pan, and spit.

When the traffic thinned out, I quit and delivered a paper around the corner to my friend Mike in his projectionist booth in the Japanese movie theater. He drinks Cokes and spikes them from a half pint. Then he says, "Three bags full!" so loud I think the audience below will hear him. Once I asked what he meant. He said he didn't get paid enough to be a slave. Then he told me how, during the war, the government put him and his family in a Japanese camp in California. But first, they kept them in the stables at Santa Anita Race Track. It sounded stupid. They put the horses some place else, I guess.

I like hanging out with Mike. He lets me watch movies from a square hole in the wall. It's usually boring because I don't know Japanese. Tonight, the actors just stood around, talking. A fight would have been good.

This time, going down Mike's familiar stairs to the street, I held on to the rail. It was always dark and smelled musty. Now it felt creepy. One step at a time, I thought. Out on the sidewalk it was dark and cold and windy. I walked up the street to catch the Red Car back to Echo Park. I could have hiked home, but I'd feel safer on a Red Car, and the icy drizzle on my face was giving me the chills. I used my eyes in the back of my head, watching for Nutso. Once, I saw a shadowy figure dodge behind people on the sidewalk.

So I ran for the Red Car up ahead taking on tons of people at the safety zone. Inside, it was crowded and steamy and the big electric motors were throbbing under the floor. I was squished up front with the dank smells of people wet from rain crawling up my nose. I looked for

Nutso, but I wasn't tall enough to see anything but arms and elbows poking me. I figured Pat Novak was short, too. Two men hung their hands on the silver seat handle next to me. There was room for me to hook a finger around the handle to stay on my feet as the Red Car rolled and swayed down Sunset. The big wipers on the front windows squeaked a steady rhythm.

I got off at Echo Park Avenue in a light rain visible in the bright neons of shops and cafes and under the streetlights. A lot of people came through the car doors in the safety zone. They were just wet shadows under their dark umbrellas.

I crossed to the old Pioneer Market building looking shiny new in the rain. The House of Spirits was built into the wall of the market. Through the fogged windows the people inside looked blurry, like I had been drinking. In my mind, Pat Novak laughed.

I went inside and the radio was playing the song "To Each His Own," making me kind of sad. I bought candy bars, a Batman comic, and ran back to Sunset. Nobody watching me that I could see. I checked it out with Pat Novak, but he said rainy nights are the worst and you couldn't be sure. I hoped I could make it home. I ran the red light across Sunset and past the Holly movie theater where I spent Saturday afternoons. The marquee read MURDER IS MY BUSINESS.

The rain in my shoes was icy and I couldn't feel my toes. I ducked up my street toward the lake and saw that my house was dark. Dad wasn't home yet. I ran inside and put on the lights, checking out the dark corners.

I turned on the radio in the living room, hoping I wasn't too late for the *Pat Novak For Hire* mystery. When Dad and Mom were home, Dad would turn out all the lights and screw in a red light bulb so we could sit together and feel spooky while we listened.

In the kitchen I could hear the news ending while I heated a can of tomato soup. Another Red Car Murder. A gangster was found tonight by the tracks in the Hollywood terminal. Shot about noon. I felt really bad that I wasn't brave enough to give the gun to Dotty. I put the gun in the tool drawer in the kitchen.

Pat Novak came on the radio and got himself hired and was creeping around in the night and fog doing his job while my soup was heating. Hearing his actual voice on the radio gave me the gumption to pull the curtains aside from the living room front windows. Rain whipping around under the traffic light. The usual shadows. The soup smelled good. I put the spread from the sofa over my shoulders and began to feel warm, in charge, almost grown up.

At the dining room table, I ate my candy bars and warmed my nose over the hot soup sitting next to my BB gun. I wished Pat Novak was really here, but he was worse off than I was. On the radio, guys were shooting at him like crazy. It would have been better if Dad or Mom were here.

I heard a sudden creak on the back porch. I turned the radio down, but not all the way, because I needed to keep Pat Novak with me. I picked up my BB gun, the metal cold in my hands. I moved softly through the kitchen.

Nobody was at the back door window. I flipped on the outside light and stepped outside with my BB gun. Even with the light, the yard looked dark and different in the rain. Not safe. The sound I'd heard was probably a dog, and I liked that possibility. I followed the dark path around the side of the house, smelling the wet geraniums, and stepping over toads going for walks, as I crept my way to the front of the house. Pat Novak was still talking in my living room, and I felt pretty good about it.

I went inside through the front door and closed it, and my heart stuck in my throat. The nutso guy with the big black beard was sitting at my dining room table, eating peanuts.

"You get out of here." I regretted my little voice and raised my BB gun.

"Kid, I want to talk to you." He snapped his wallet open and shut. I guessed he was showing me something. "Special Agent John Roop, Pacific Electric."

He was a piss-poor looking special agent. More like a rogue cop. I figured a rogue cop wouldn't take good care of himself and this was him. No knock on the door. Didn't ask to come in. I figured he saw me put his gun in my pocket, take the dynamite caps, and not pay the motorman. He wanted his gun back so he could kill me to stop me from telling on him.

"Good looking BB gun you got there," he said. "Kid, I'm looking into the Red Car Murders. Are your parents home?"

"My dad and mom are cooking supper," I said.

He looked around the dining room as if to see them, and nodded.

My BB gun was pointed at his belly. "You don't look like a special agent." I checked to see if the gun was cocked.

"I'm undercover." He tilted his head at the radio, listening, as Pat Novak was trying to talk his way past a guy with a gun and a crazy laugh.

"Be a sport and talk to me," said Nutso.

"I'll go tell my dad you're here," I said.

"I know you're alone, kid." He crunched another peanut, studying me with blue bloodshot eyes, like he was trying to figure out how to win me over. "Looky here, I know you found something under the Red Car seat. Give it to me." He cracked more peanut shells, dropping them to the hardwood floor. My heart was pumping in my throat.

"Have a peanut?" he said, tossing one to me. It bounced off me. "I saw you climb through the window and take something from under that car seat. That doesn't have to be a problem. No fuss at all, I expect. But, it's very important that you give it to me."

Pat Novak was telling the killer to give it up, 'cause he was going to jail. Killer footsteps echoed down a hollow hallway.

The music got glad.

There was a loud knock on the front door.

"I'll get it, kid." Nutso got up and walked softly toward the front door. I followed him, raising my BB gun by the barrel over my head, and whacked him hard on the head with the wooden stock. He fell in a heap on the living room floor and lay still, peanuts rolling everywhere.

I edged the front door open. A big fist with shiny brass knuckles jammed straight through the doorway. I backed up but got some brass knuckles and a sinking pain in my face anyway and fell to the floor. I tasted blood.

"Okay, kid," said the man behind the big fist, his voice loud and scratchy, eyes like wet cement. He pulled me up, the BB gun between us, and rubbed his metal fist over my bleeding nose. It hurt so much I almost peed in my pants. His breath was close and smelled like old fish, and I wanted to vomit.

"Give me the gun, soldier, and I'll be on my way," he breathed in my face.

My lower lip was trembling, and my eyes got hot with tears. I jerked back, and my finger, still on the trigger, fired the BB gun. The barrel was pointed up and a copper BB pinged off his gold tooth.

"Shit!" The man grabbed his mouth.

I ducked back into the dining room, cocking the BB gun. I could hear him following. I grabbed my soup bowl and slung the hot tomato soup in his face.

"Jesus!" he yelled, wiping soup away from his eyes with his fingers. His face looked really bloody, but he was blinking at me and stumbling toward me. "I'm gonna kill you, you dumb little shit."

I shot a BB in his gut and ran into the kitchen. The tool drawer was open and the little silver gun was gone. My stomach felt loose.

"Mark," whispered a woman's voice. "Over here."

I looked into the dark breakfast nook, and there was Officer Dotty Sullivan in her police uniform. She motioned me toward her, then stood up and pointed my little silver gun at the man charging into the room.

"Police! Stop!" she commanded.

He kept coming and she shot him. He twisted to the floor, grabbing his leg and squeezing, yelling he was dying. Blood leaked through his fingers, though his tomato soup face looked worse off than his leg.

"I meant to shoot him in the chest," she said, sounding kind of embarrassed.

"Boy, I'm glad you're here, Dotty," I said, mopping my own bloody face with a dishtowel. "You followed me home?"

"I hung around your corner because you seemed to

have a problem. This guy was following you. I followed him. Here I am. I came through the back door, saw your tool drawer open, and found the gun. Lucky for us. LAPD won't issue guns to policewomen. No training."

That explained her aim, I thought. The guy was lucky, too.

"Hey, who's that bum on the floor at the front door?" She was peering through the dining room at Nutso.

"He says he's a special agent for the big Red Cars," I said. "But I think he's the rogue cop killing those gangsters, and you got his gun. He saw me take it from where he hid it under the Red Car seat. He's the Red Car Killer."

"Actually, I'd vote for this guy on the kitchen floor. What's your name?" she asked him.

No answer from Brass Knuckles. He was still clutching his leg and moaning.

Dotty studied him. "I'm pretty sure I've seen his mug shot, but I can't place him. Get his wallet, Mark." She pointed her gun at his head.

I hoped her aim had improved. I leaned down and pulled his wallet from his pocket. "There's no driver's license," I said.

"Joke's on you, punk," he spit. "I don't drive. I take—" He stopped.

"You take the streetcars," Dotty finished for him. "Sure. That explains why the killer took the Red Cars." She studied him again. Then she got this look, like a light bulb went on in her head. "Gutsy," she said slowly. "Gutsy Hormel." She nodded, pleased. "He was connected with gambling ships before the war. The government stopped the ships in 1939 because they were inside the three-mile limit. Gutsy ran off to Chicago.

That's where he's from. As far as I knew, he was still there."

"So why is he back in L.A.?" I asked. "And why is he killing gangsters?"

She thought some more. "There's a lot of money to be made with gambling ships. My guess? Gutsy is knocking off local gangsters so Chicago gangsters can move in and set up gambling ships way beyond the three mile limit off Santa Monica bay." She glanced at him. "Apparently, old Gutsy never learned to drive. No good with cars or ships, or kids. Poor sap."

Gutsy snarled and tried to move away.

"Stay where you are," Dotty ordered. "I have to call the station," she told me, keeping the gun and her eyes on Gutsy while reaching with her free hand for the telephone on the kitchen wall.

Nutso let out a big groan in the living room. I grabbed another dishtowel and ran over to him. He was sitting up and touching the back of his head with his hands. I gave him the towel.

"Thanks, kid."

"Hey, are you a real special agent?"

He nodded and winced, touching the towel to the back of his head. "Where's that bastard who hit me?"

"That was me," I said. "I'm sorry. I thought you were the Red Car Murderer."

He eyed me. "You're pretty strong for a kid. Glad to know you're on my side now."

I couldn't tell if he was mad or not. "Hey, you're beard's falling off."

He caught it and stuffed it in his coat pocket, but most of it flopped outside, like a small critter trying to escape.

"So, what was under that streetcar seat?" Nutso rose to his feet.

"The killer's gun," I said.

"Kid, that's why I'm here." He sighed. "Are you going to help me or give me the runaround?"

"We got the killer in the kitchen," I said. "Officer Dotty shot him in the leg. She's calling the station, so more cops are coming."

In the kitchen, Nutso held his badge out for Dotty, who was fixing a tourniquet on the leg of the Red Car murderer.

"I'm John Roop, Pacific Electric Special Agent. Undercover on the Red Car Murders. Your guy on the kitchen floor chucked something under the car seat when he saw me coming. I guess he made me. He sat up front, watching me. Before I could check out the seat, this kid crashed through the car window, took the killer's gun, jumped ship and zipped down Sunset. I followed him. Looks like this guy followed the kid, too. Know who he is?"

"Lester 'Gutsy' Hormel," Dotty said. "He—"

"Mark!"

I jumped. It was my dad's voice.

"Turn that damn radio down!" He was standing in the front doorway, shaking the rain off his umbrella.

Jesus Happy Christ. Dad was back!

"Sounds like a goddamned circus," said Dad as he crossed into the dining room and stopped, staring at me and Nutso standing like buddies in the kitchen doorway. I don't think he saw behind us in the kitchen where Dotty was still working on Gutsy's leg. My nose was bleeding again, and I wiped it easy like with the towel.

"We got company, I see." said Dad.

I turned the radio down a bit, wondering why he was taking it so well. Dad put his hand on my shoulder and examined my sore nose. "Been roughhousing, huh?" He leaned over and whispered. "Mark, we got a phone call from your mom. She's coming home on the train. She says we're a helluva lot more fun than the hog farm."

The music on the radio got glad.

"Dad, wait till you see what's in the kitchen."

On the radio, Pat Novak said, "I'd do it again." His feet crunched gravel and a bunch of foghorns growled out in San Francisco bay.

Continuing northwesterly on a link of Sunset that was once part of historic Route 66, we're coming to the neighborhood of Silver Lake. Note the vintage houses, many designed by L.A.'s resident architectural A-list, perched on the sides of green hills, approachable only by the steep, narrow streets and the impossibly long staircases that provided backdrops for numerous comedy films of the 1930s. The jewel of the area is Silver Lake itself, a reservoir, actually, which offers views unmatched anywhere in the Los Angeles area. And like the lake itself, the neighborhood maintains an atmosphere of peace and tranquility. But also like the lake, stronger, perhaps even dangerous, currents might lurk just underneath the surface...

EXTREME PREJUDICE

by Dale Furutani

"I think it's disgusting that a man like that should be allowed near young children."

"Whatever are you talking about?"

"Haven't you noticed how he pays special attention to children, talking to them all the time and giving them candy and such?"

"But Mr. Johnson is a retired school bus driver. He knows some of those children, at least the older ones. He used to drive them to school when they were in kindergarten."

I put down my mystery book and listened more closely. Ivory Johnson was a friend of mine.

"Yes, but look how he uses that fancy car to lure children to him." She dropped her voice to a hoarse whisper that still carried to me as I sat in my backyard, hidden behind the tall wooden fence that encircled it. "Especially the white ones!"

I heard a sigh. I was sure that was Vera Dodd. I was also pretty sure who was slandering Ivory.

"Really!" Mrs. Dodd said. "You shouldn't say such things, Marigold Baker. It's not nice and I'm sure it's not true."

Marigold Baker. I was right about who was saying nasty things about Ivory.

"Hrumpphh," Mrs. Baker said. "You just go ahead and keep your head in the sand. When some child is found violated or murdered, you just remember this conversation!"

I heard Mrs. Baker walk rapidly away, her heels clicking against the sidewalk in staccato anger. I don't know when Vera Dodd walked away because she was probably wearing walking shoes like any sensible person out for a stroll.

My house sits on a corner, about a block from Silver Lake Reservoir. Because of this, people walk by it all the time as they stroll or jog around the reservoir. Sitting or working in my yard I often hear people passing by, eavesdropping on snatches of conversation or perhaps hearing the jingle of a choke chain if they're leading a dog. Yet, in almost thirty years in my house, I had never heard a conversation more upsetting.

Agitated and angry, I closed my book and got out of my chair. I thought Mrs. Baker was being a racist. Perhaps I don't have the right to say such harsh things, but Japanese believe that once you're past sixty-one you can pretty much say what you like. At my age, I view sixty-one as the days when I was young, so I've more than earned whatever privileges come with longevity.

I walked over to the potting bench in the shaded area of my yard and told myself to calm down. Picking up one of my favorite bonsai, I looked at it critically from all angles. It was a tiny grove of three pomegranate trees, with the tallest tree only eight inches high. I put it down and got my shears and gloves out of the plastic fishing tackle box under the potting bench.

I took a deep breath and tried to bring myself into balance. You should be calm when working on a bonsai so you don't make mistakes. In this case, I was forcing myself to be calm by starting work instead of starting work when I was calm.

On a good bonsai, nothing is left unconsidered. Each bend of a limb, each needle or leaf, each patch of moss around the base is carefully thought out. If nature doesn't provide what the bonsai artist wants, then the artist must fashion it, using carefully bent copper wire or selective nurturing or the snip of a shear. Without this sculpturing and nurturing, all you have is a small plant, not a bonsai.

Some day my pomegranate grove will be a miniature world of beauty, encircled in an oval dish. The trees will bear red fruit that is only an inch across. The moss at the base of the trees will be flecked with gold highlights and a few artfully placed pebbles will look like rugged boulders. It will be a perfect little world, unmarred by human pettiness and bigotry. It will be a world unlike the one that stretches away from the edge of my fence.

Silver Lake is a multi-ethnic community in the heart of Los Angeles. In a city where neighborhoods are usually segregated by race, this is fairly rare. Ivory Johnson is a black man, but he is just one of many African-Americans, Latinos, Asians and whites, both gay and straight, who live in this neighborhood. I'm included in that list, by the way; the straight Asian part of it, anyway.

My name is Shig Ogawa and I guess I'm sort of a stereotype. You guessed it—I'm a Japanese gardener. Like a lot of stereotypes, this one hasn't been modified by the passage of time, but the truth is that you rarely find a Japanese American working as a gardener anymore. This profession, at least in Los Angeles, is now filled with Latinos, Vietnamese and the occasional Korean. They do it for the same reasons we did it. When you're starting out in America, gardening is a business that allows you to substitute sweat for capital. When I got out of the relocation camp after World War II, my options were pretty limited, so I took up gardening as a profession. My kids went to UCLA and UC Santa Barbara, and one is a CPA and the other a businesswoman. I'm proud of them and proud that they won't have to haul groaning bags of heavy grass clippings on days when the temperature is 105.

Don't get me wrong. I like gardening. It represents hope for the future when you plant something that may not grow and blossom for years. It's just that it's hard work and it takes a long time to make any money doing it. Now that I'm retired and don't have to put two kids through college, I do gardening for pleasure.

I put down the shears and stopped working. The world outside my borders had disturbed my harmony too much to work on a bonsai. I went in the house, put on some better clothes, and went to see Ivory Johnson.

Ivory lived a few blocks away. As usual, he was outside his apartment polishing his Jaguar XK150.

This car was his pride and joy—a cream-colored convertible with tan leather interior. It was the model made before the famous XKE Jaguar. You could tell the sporty lineage in the swooping fenders and the big, inline six-cylinder engine. If Ivory wasn't fussing with the outside of the car, he had his head under the tiny hood tinkering with the engine. "Same basic engine they raced at LeMans," he'd tell you with pride. "SU carburetors and overhead cams. Clark Gable owned one of these!" Then he'd beam, as if owning the same kind of car as Gable made him a movie star, too.

Myself, I preferred a nice big pickup truck, but I

always viewed automobiles as another tool of my trade, like a sturdy lawnmower or a good rake, not some kind of plaything.

"Hi, Ivory," I said.

"Shig, my man, come look at this!" He pointed proudly at the large steering wheel that dominated the cockpit of the car. I studied it, not knowing what I was supposed to be seeing. It seemed to me that it was an old wheel and, as I remembered it, Ivory's car used to have a much fancier steering wheel made of chrome and wood.

"It's nice," I said tentatively.

"Nice? Shig, that's an original XK150 steering wheel. Before I got this great automobile, a previous owner replaced the steering wheel with a Nardi. The Nardi's a nice looking wheel, but it's not original. Everything else is original, so not having the right steering wheel bugged me. I searched all over and finally found one in a wrecking yard in Indiana. It took a few long distance phone calls and a chunk of my next pension check, but this little baby is mine!" He caressed the wheel fondly, like a younger man might caress a lover.

"I just came back from a nice drive on Sunset. It's my favorite trip. I start at the bridge on Silver Lake Boulevard. Do you know it?"

Of course I knew it. Around here Sunset crosses two bridges, although I doubt if most people driving on Sunset realize it. They allow Glendale Boulevard and Silver Lake Boulevard to pass under Sunset. You have to take a small side street to go from Silver Lake to Sunset.

"Anyway, I started at the bridge and drove the entire length of Sunset. I went past the Sunset Strip and the fancy homes by UCLA. Then I continued all the way to Pacific Palisades and the ocean. It was a great trip with the top down and the wind caressing my face. I was celebrating and testing out my new steering wheel. Now the car is done. Completely restored. This old steering wheel is the final touch, the olive in the martini, the jewel in the crown!" He looked at me and I almost thought he was going to cry. "Just in time, too, Shig," he continued. "I've just found out I'm going blind." Then he did cry.

We spent the afternoon sitting on the porch in front of Ivory's apartment, drinking beer and cheering each other up by complaining about what hell it was to grow old. Ivory talked about his heart problems and I talked about my arthritis. Strangely, we didn't talk much about Ivory going blind. He did say he went to the UCLA eye clinic for a check-up because his vision was getting blurry. That's where he got the sad news. The degeneration of his eyesight was hereditary and it was progressive. In a short time he'd be legally blind and in a few years he'd be completely blind. It gave me pause, especially since I knew it was a situation I'd have to face some day. Not the blindness, maybe, but the knowledge that some day I wouldn't be able to take care of myself and I'd have to figure out what I was going to do.

My wife Michiko died five years ago. It had never occurred to me that I would outlive her. She was younger than me, but cancer doesn't select its victims chronologically. When I thought of being incapacitated by old age, it had always been in terms of not being a burden to my kids. I still wasn't going to be a burden to my kids, but now when I considered how I was going to end my days, it was in terms of nursing homes or hospitals, not staying at home with Michiko.

Ivory and I didn't get drunk, but we both drank a few more beers than we were used to and my head was swimming when I walked home. I never did mention the horrible things Marigold Baker said.

A few days later, there was a knock on my door. I opened it to reveal a young girl, maybe eighteen or nineteen, standing on my doorstep. She had long black hair that hung down straight and she wore a flowered blouse, vest, blue jeans, and clunky boots. She sort of looked like my daughter did in the sixties, although she wasn't Asian. You know you're old when even your kid's fashions are recycled by a successive generation.

"Yes?" I asked.

"Excuse me, sir. My name is Jill and we're going around the neighborhood to see if there are any odd jobs, repairs or errands you'd like run."

I looked past her to see who "we" were and saw a sullen, thin, redheaded boy standing on the sidewalk, looking at us. His beard was scraggly and he had on a T-shirt, blue jeans, and black boots. On his skinny bicep was a tattoo of a snake crawling out of the eye-socket of a skull. I saw why the girl had been chosen to come to the door. Silver Lake is a friendly neighborhood, but it's still in Los Angeles, the home of the big hustle. As you get snow on the roof, people think your brain has leached out into the gray hair, so they target older people especially. I did have a few odd jobs I wanted done but I wasn't about to invite two strangers into my home to do them and told her I didn't have any work.

A few days after that, I saw the couple hard at work polishing Ivory's Jaguar. I had to grudgingly admit they looked like they were putting a lot of elbow grease into it, really making that car gleam. I saw them around Ivory's place increasingly after that. Sometimes they'd be doing odd jobs or gardening, other times they'd be working on that darned car of Ivory's. Ivory told me he got the landlord to pay the couple for most of their work and he subsidized the rest, especially the car stuff. Once I even saw the boy, whose name was Tim, driving the car with a smiling Ivory sitting in the passenger's seat. It saddened me to think that soon this would be the only way Ivory would be able to enjoy his car, just riding in the passenger's seat.

Despite the constant presence of the couple at Ivory's, I was surprised a few weeks later when Ivory made an announcement to me. I bumped into him in the produce section of the local Mayfair supermarket and he said, "I'm letting them move in with me, Shig."

"Who?"

"Tim and Jill."

"That couple you've been helping out?"

"Yep. They live in a crummy apartment down near Sunset and come up to Silver Lake every day to look for work. I've got a big apartment with an extra bedroom. I used to use it as a kind of library, but the truth is I can't see well enough to read anymore."

"Do you know much about them?" I asked doubtfully.

"What's there to know? They're good kids, Shig. They work hard. Tim is sitting in the car in the parking lot right now, waiting for me to get done. They've just had some bad breaks in life. Maybe I can help them get a new start."

"But bringing strangers into your home..."

Ivory laughed. "Come on, Shig, you've got to loosen up. I want to give the kids a chance. Besides," he said, lowering his voice, "my eyesight is deteriorating even faster now and if they're living with me it will make it easier when I finally go blind."

When you get older, some people start treating you like a child, so I wasn't about to do that to Ivory. He was intelligent and a man I respected, so I bit my tongue and didn't voice any of the reservations I felt about his decision.

Despite my misgivings, Jill and Tim living at Ivory's seemed to work out. They continued to work hard, getting new odd jobs around the neighborhood and forming a little family with Ivory. I knew Ivory had married twice, but neither time took and he didn't have any kids. I didn't know much about the rest of his family, except that they lived in Alabama. So maybe the young couple filled a void in his life.

One day I went over to Ivory's apartment and was surprised to see Jill sitting on his porch, reading a book. I had pictured her as a TV watcher, not a reader. I felt a pang of guilt. Maybe Ivory was right and I needed to loosen up and put more faith in people. If I didn't watch it, in my own way I might end up as sour as Marigold Baker.

"Hi," I said.

Jill looked up from her book. "Oh, hi," she answered.

"What are you reading?"

"One of Mr. Johnson's books. It's all about spies and stuff. It's pretty interesting." She pointed to the open book. "For instance, do you know what spies call it when they kill off someone?"

"Assassination?"

"Nope. They say they're going to eliminate someone with extreme prejudice. Isn't that cool?"

"Yes, it is," I agreed. "So much more sophisticated than saying you're going to murder someone. Very sanitary."

She gave me a puzzled look and I decided to change the subject. "Is Ivory around?"

"Yeah. He's in the back with Tim, working on the car."

What else? I made my way to the back where Ivory had his garage. I found him and the young man hard at work. The kid was using swabs to clean the spokes of the Jaguar's wire wheels and Ivory was wiping down the finish with a soft cloth.

"Hi, Ivory," I said. I nodded to the young man and acknowledged him with a "Tim." He sort of grunted and continued his work with the swab. I pointed to him and said to Ivory, "That's a little much, even for you, cleaning things with swabs. What are you going to do, enter the car in a contest or something?"

"Shig, my man!" He laughed. "No, no contest. Something even better. I'm going to sell the car."

I was stunned. I looked at him and blinked, but he just continued to look in my direction and didn't seem to see my surprise. "Are you sure?" I asked.

"Oh yes. Let's take a break, Tim," he said, putting down the polishing rag. He dug into his pocket and pulled out a candy bar. He tossed it in the general direction of Tim, who caught it and started unwrapping it with obvious relish. Ivory still enjoyed handing out candy. He walked out of the garage to me, reaching out to touch me like he was afraid he'd run into me if he didn't. He sighed. "It's just time, Shig. My eyesight is so bad I can't even see the dashboard. Things are just hazy shapes now. Besides, Tim thinks we should get a new sedan or something because my car is really too valuable to be used for running down to the Mayfair for a quart of milk."

"That car is worth a lot of money?"

Ivory laughed. "You'd be surprised, Shig. Tim and Jill did all the research and work about what the market is like and I'm giving them a ten percent commission for their help."

"Are you selling it through an auction or a dealer?"

"Neither. We've got an ad appearing in several specialty newspapers for car collectors. We're going to handle it all ourselves. That's why Tim and Jill are getting the commission."

"Isn't that dangerous? I've heard stories of cars being bought with phony cashier's checks and things like that."

Ivory laughed again. "Always looking for the worst! Shig, you've got to stop reading those mystery books because they're making you suspicious of everything."

"But..."

Ivory put up his hand. "Okay, I know you're right, but Tim had a great idea to stop that. We're going to make the buyer give us cash for the car."

"Cash?"

"I'll put it in the bank, but I think it would be fun to have that much cash in my hands, just once."

"But Ivory..."

"It's all right, Shig. I know what I'm doing."

A week later, I saw a flatbed truck go past my house with Ivory's prize Jaguar sitting on it and I knew Ivory had sold his car.

The next morning, Ivory was dead.

If the timing had been different, things might have also turned out differently, but Ivory died on the morning I left to spend a couple of weeks with my daughter in Santa Barbara. A neighbor found him in his apartment and the police said it was a heart attack. I didn't find out about it until I got home.

I was shocked and upset by the news, but not so shocked that I didn't immediately make the connection between the cash for the Jaguar and Ivory's sudden death.

Trying to convince the authorities that my suspicions were more than an old man's paranoia was frustrating. I called the police, but I didn't know how much Ivory got for the Jaguar or who he sold it to or have proof that he had died of anything but natural causes.

A detective could have solved all these things, I suppose, but I wasn't a detective. You could hunt down the Jaguar buyer through the change in title with the Department of Motor Vehicles and find out how much he or she paid for the car and if it really was in cash. Then you could get permission from Ivory's relatives, who were all in Alabama, to have an autopsy performed.

I explained all this to a nice lady detective from the Northeast Division of the Los Angeles Police Department but I got the distinct impression that she thought my complaint was bunk. Los Angeles is so huge, so full of problems, and so under-policed that it almost takes a murder in progress while you're calling to get any attention. Ivory was an old man and it's not unusual for old men to die in their sleep, especially if they have a heart condition like Ivory did. Well, I'm an old man and I can tell you I'll find it unusual if someone shortens my life by even one minute, if it isn't my time to go.

Frustrated, I wasn't sure what to do next, but, surprisingly enough, the Los Angeles Department of Water and Power, the DWP, provided a resolution to my dilemma.

Every ten to fifteen years, the DWP gets big ideas

about Silver Lake Reservoir. Once they wanted to cover it and another time they wanted to rebuild the dam and dramatically reduce its size. When this happens, the Silver Lake community gets together and organizes itself to collectively kick the DWP's butt. Then peace reigns for a while, until a new management team arrives at the DWP and new plans are drawn for the reservoir. Then we start over again.

This time the DWP wanted to build a water filtration plant right by the lakeside. There's a perfectly good site in an industrial area just a short distance from the reservoir. The community contended it would actually be cheaper for the DWP to build the plant there instead of by the lake because they wouldn't need to spend a lot of money shielding it from the neighborhood. But, as with any bureaucracy, once a large organization gets an idea, it's almost impossible to change it. So the community was going to hire its own engineering team to cost out the two plants to show which one would be cheaper. This, of course, required money.

I volunteered to help raise money and the community association assigned me to canvass Moreno Drive and Kenilworth Avenue. I swore I'd knock on every door, despite the fact there are some doors I'd probably prefer skipping. Silver Lake diversity extends to having a few kooks and cranks in the neighborhood, too.

The streets of Silver Lake are twisting and very hilly. Despite that, it was a pleasant walk as I made my way from house to house, knocking on doors and going into my little patter about the lake and the need for money.

The people were receptive and, contrary to my expectations, I was actually enjoying myself. So, when I came to Marigold Baker's house, I decided I wouldn't renege on my promise to knock on every door. I marched up and smartly rang the doorbell.

I was stunned when Jill answered the door.

If she recognized me, she didn't reveal it. Maybe we do all look alike, but I think her lack of recognition had more to do with me being old than being Asian. The very young don't look too closely at the very old.

"Yeah?" she asked.

I stumbled a bit as my mind raced ahead. Should I excuse myself and call the police? Would the police come, since I really didn't have any evidence? When she didn't recognize me, I decided just to go into my pitch and figure out what to do after I left her.

"I'm here collecting donations to preserve the lake," I started. "We need to do a study to show that building an off-site filtration plant is actually cheaper than a lakeside…"

"Oh, just a minute," she said, interrupting me. She closed the door and disappeared. I stood awkwardly on the doorstep and wondered what I should do. I was about to leave when the door opened again.

"Here," Jill said, thrusting a bill at me. "Mrs. Baker says good luck with your cause." Then she closed the door.

It was a twenty. I looked at it for several minutes, as if I had never seen one before. As Andrew Jackson's face stared back at me, I knew something was terribly wrong. I looked around the front of the house and saw a wooden gate leading into the back. I walked over, opened the latch, and hurried down the side of the house.

I got into the backyard and even in my haste I couldn't help but look around in disgust. The lawn was brown and shot through with weeds and the flower border was a straggly disgrace. An old rusted barbecue stood forlornly in the corner. I know it was a strange thing to notice while I was sneaking around in Mrs. Baker's backyard, but it was just the gardener in me.

At the back of the house were a couple of windows that looked like they might be for a bedroom. The curtain was drawn back. I wondered if I should look in. I could just hear Mrs. Baker's screech if she caught me and I wasn't sure the police would accept seeing Jill and getting twenty dollars as a good enough reason for turning into a Peeping Tom. Then I thought of Ivory and steeled myself to peek inside, regardless of the consequences.

I looked into Marigold Baker's bedroom. The furniture was so old it was fashionable again. A dresser stood along one wall and a bed along the other. Lounging in the doorway of the bedroom, taking in everything with an interested eye, was Jill. On the bed were Marigold Baker and Tim. Mrs. Baker was lying on her back and Tim was sitting on top of her, using his knees to pin down her arms. In his hands was a pillow and he was pushing it into her face.

I looked around the yard again, desperate. I ran over and picked up the barbecue. It was surprisingly heavy, but urgency gave me power. I swung the barbecue back and heaved it at the window with all my strength.

It hit the window with an explosion of splintering glass. Both Tim and Jill looked up, astounded.

"I'm calling the police," I shouted. "She'd better be alive when they get here!"

I'm not as spry and fast as I used to be but I was fast enough to get out of there and make good on my threat.

A few days later, I was sitting in my yard again, thinking about the incident, and feeling pretty good about myself. It turned out that the police had actually been making some inquiries into Ivory's death. When they interviewed Tim and Jill, they claimed they had moved out of Ivory's apartment a few days before he died. An old man with a heart condition dying alone is not suspicious, but a young couple hurriedly moving out to make it seem like the old man died alone is a red flag even to an overworked police department like L.A.'s. They pledged to kick the investigation of Ivory's death into high gear because of Tim and Jill's attempted murder of Mrs. Baker.

Of course, knowing Marigold Baker, it was obvious something was drastically wrong when I got a twenty dollar donation. It's not nice of me to say this, but Marigold Baker wouldn't spit on a man dying of thirst, much less give twenty dollars to some neighborhood cause. To get rid of me before I saw or heard something, Jill had just grabbed a bill off the pile of money she and Tim had somehow conned Mrs. Baker into withdrawing from her savings.

I glanced over at my bonsai bench and felt in the mood to work on my pomegranates again. Before I could get up, I heard Vera Dodd's voice.

"Oh, Marigold, I heard about the terrible thing that happened to you! I'm glad to see you're up and about."

"Yes. It was awful! I don't know how those children fooled me. They seemed so helpful and nice," Mrs. Baker said.

"Well, I'm glad you're okay, thanks to Mr. Ogawa."

"Hrumpphh!"

"Why, what's the matter, Marigold?"

"You know, that man broke my window and didn't even offer to pay for it! I should sue him. That damn Jap."

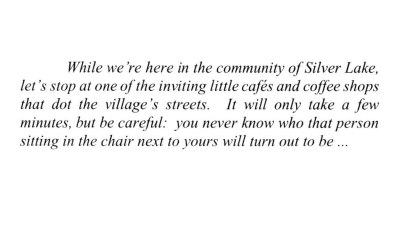

While we're here in the community of Silver Lake, let's stop at one of the inviting little cafés and coffee shops that dot the village's streets. It will only take a few minutes, but be careful: you never know who that person sitting in the chair next to yours will turn out to be ...

THREE KILLINGS AND A FAVOR

By Joan Waites

Romeo Carlos de Jesus is not a man you meet on the way up, understand? He's blown up cars and burned down houses, shot people in the face, stabbed, beaten and poisoned traitorous men, unfaithful women and annoying pets. So when he comes sauntering up to me while I'm sitting in the park, fear slams through me like an 18-wheeler. It constricts my breath, brings heat to my face and makes my fingertips tingle, like when you're driving and realize that you're about to smash into something. I figure this is it, I'm going down, *all the way down*, to be tortured for eternity and made to crave ice water.

I could scramble over the bench and up the hill into the shrubs, but he'd shoot me in the back. I could dodge him and run forward, dive into the lake, but he'd follow me and drown me there. I could leap upon him and scratch at his eyes, bite his nose like they showed us way back when in self-defense class, but he'd mace me with my own pepper spray and stab me in the gut. So I sit. Rub my sweaty hands against my pale blue skirt. And I wait, endlessly it seems, while he lopes across the green, green grass and finally slows to a stop in front of me.

"I understand, *guera*, that you are in some trouble, no?" His voice is rich and calm and throaty. His accent is pronounced. He rolls his R's and speaks slowly.

I slit my eyes at him. My throat is to dry too respond even if I had something to say.

"The Cabrera brothers, they tell me you have seen a thing not meant for your eyes. Some guns. In a barrel you thought would contain hazardous waste. No?"

He is close enough that I can smell him, not cologne or aftershave but the scent of Romeo himself, an earthy, promising scent. It is everything I can do to keep from shaking. The strain of keeping still leaves me unable to stop the tears.

Romeo closes his eyes and shakes his head, smiling. "No, no, no, *señorita*. No need for tears. When it comes it will be painless. That was what the brothers requested."

He pulls a Kool menthol cigarette from the pack rolled up in his sleeve, replaces the pack. I notice his jeans. They fit him in that impossible way jeans do in the ads, tight in the ass and crumpled, but not baggy, everywhere else. These are over black work boots. He pulls a lighter from these incredible jeans and lights the cigarette, then slides the lighter back into his pocket.

He is a handsome man, this Romeo de Jesus. But he is a killer. He is not much past my twenty-three years, just thirty, I think. I know him, or rather know *of* him, from the waste treatment plant where I work. He comes in and has conversations with the Cabrera brothers. They speak in Spanish. I understand little of this exotic language and I'm glad for it. Certain things are not disguised by a language barrier, and I don't want to hear specifics.

Romeo takes a luxurious drag from his menthol, blows the smoke in a stream that reminds me of a dragon. He assesses me. I swallow. He pulls the cigarette from his mouth and offers it to me. I smoked only briefly, in college, but I appreciate the gesture and accept.

Romeo lights another for himself, then sits down close to me on the bench. We sit like that for a long while, smoking in silence like old friends and staring out over Silver Lake. Then he says, "Tell me your name, *señorita.*"

"They didn't tell you?'"

"Of course they did. But I want to hear you say it. It's different when a woman speaks her own name than when a man repeats it." He smiles.

"Sarah. Sarah Bradstone."

"And your middle name?"

"Ramona."

"Well, *Señorita* Sarah Ramona Bradstone, I am telling you that I am not generally in the business of killing little girls for making mistakes at work." He grins. "First thing, the Cabrera brothers tell me: the man who carelessly included such a drum with a regular legitimate shipment, kill him. I check and I find that this man has repeatedly been warned about just this very offense many times, and also evidence that he is a snitch. So I kill him."

He grins again. It starts me shaking and this time I can't control it. Any minute I'm expecting his gun to my temple, cool and deadly. He carries it tucked in his waistband in the back. His T-shirt is loose over the top of it, but you can see it if you look.

He sets a hand on my back and I jump. He shakes his head like before. "Let me finish."

I nod, finishing my cigarette and rubbing it out against the wood of the park bench.

"Here is what they tell me next," Romeo says. "They tell me a girl has seen their trade, their guns, and they don't know what to do. I tell them; pretend it's not yours! No, they say. Too late. Kill her. So I check and I find that this girl's first job from college is working with these Cabrera brothers. These are bad men, and she is greener than the unripe jalapeño, this little Sarah Ramona Bradstone."

His dark eyes hold my gaze. My mouth opens but I say nothing.

His voice is low and velvety. "I tell them I will not take this job. They do not like that answer. They threaten me and make black promises against me."

Romeo sits back against the bench and crosses his feet at the ankles. He clasps his hands behind his head and looks up at the sky. It's a big, blue, cloudless sky and he sighs, contentedly.

"Dying men tell the truth. I am telling you to go home and pack a bag, and we will put you on a plane."

* * *

"Is this you?" Romeo holds a framed photograph of a curvy blonde in a green dress.

"No, that's Madeline, my sister."

"Are you sure? She looks just like you." He laughs gently. "If I came and she were here, I would kill her and think I'd killed you."

I cringe at this, but more because I'm expected to by polite society than because it really bothers me. It *should* bother me. But it doesn't. Like his not needing directions from Silver Lake to my place in Hollywood should have bothered me and didn't. He drove me right down Sunset in his sexy black Porsche, oblivious to the envious stares of people on the sidewalks. He knew what street to turn on. And he got lucky, found parking just two blocks away.

Thinking of parking reminds me. "Madeline is

stopping by for coffee today!"

"At what time?"

"After her shop closes. Usually around six."

"You should not say goodbye. But probably you must. Just do not tell her where you are going. Otherwise, I have wasted my favor on you." He smiles. It is a fond and trusting smile.

I return to ransacking my closet, trying to decide what I should bring to wear for the rest of my life in New York. Romeo is on my cordless telephone, ordering a ticket and using a credit card, *his* credit card, to pay. He meanders here and there through my sunny little one-bedroom apartment, examining everything in a way that reminds me of a cat. Every time he moves toward me I'm expecting his gun. I'm not convinced he's even on the phone. I think he's just holding it to his ear as a prop, trying to calm me down so he can sneak up from behind. Panic keeps rising in my chest and I breathe, breathe, breathe to fight it back.

I stuff a black dress into the single remaining corner of my duffel. I am wrestling it closed when Romeo gets off the phone and helps. "Tonight, at eleven-fifty, your plane takes off," he tells me.

I glance at my Bettie Page clock. Her little pitchfork's on the four and her long devil's tail is just past the six. "Lotta time between now and then."

"Do not worry, we will spend it. And we will be home at seven so you can have coffee with your sister. Are you hungry? I am hungry. What would you like to eat?"

Last Supper, is what I'm thinking but I keep this to myself. "There's a Cajun place up the street a ways. We could walk there."

He nods approval and we set off, up my street to La

Cienega, then up the hill to Sunset.

A place appears different once you know you are about to leave it. I stand waiting for the light to change and gaze down this street I have lived on or near since I came here five years ago to go to UCLA. It suddenly looks to me as it did the first time I saw it, fantastic and impossible with its billboards and television screens, larger than life images and naked, gender-ambiguous models. Have I really lived here five years? Is there actually a man standing next to me who should and might murder me before the day is up? A shudder runs through me.

Romeo has a way of keeping near me, like a possessive boyfriend. There was no question of who would drive from Silver Lake; my Honda is abandoned there. And there was his pacing in the apartment. I never would have made it past him out my door. Now he stands close behind me, propped against the light pole with one lean, muscular arm, so that he'd easily block me if I were to try to run.

We say almost nothing in the fifteen minutes it takes to get to the restaurant, The Cajun Bistro. Romeo's keys are clipped to his belt loop and jangle rhythmically as he walks. Once there, we sit on the patio and watch the people go past. He sits next to me rather than across the table, and I can smell the heat coming off him. I order a glass of wine, I think I can use it. Romeo asks for iced tea. We both get the shrimp jambalaya.

I am still very much afraid of Romeo. I am still convinced he will put a bullet in my head before the end of the day. Maybe on the way to the airport. *Probably*, I've decided. But something, the wine perhaps? The calmness of the man and his promise of no pain? Something has made me distance myself from this grim reality of imminent death. I'm relaxed and at peace. New York or hell, it's all the same.

The sun is beginning to drop and the sky is spread with deep tones of evening. It has been a mild spring day, the kind that breeds both restlessness and complacency, often in the same soul. We both gaze skyward for a long while.

"It's nice to be out," I say.

Romeo nods. "Not such a bad day to die."

This is it. Panic runs through me in a hot streak, despite my momentary acceptance. I flinch and pull away.

But from nothing. There is no weapon, only Romeo's easy smile. "The *señorita* misunderstands me," he says in his velvet voice, R's rolling.

He waits for me to compose myself. As I do so I see him differently. There is a veiled sadness apparent in his face, and a strange, new urgency in his eyes.

He peers down Sunset Boulevard. "I told you that a dying man tells the truth. Let me tell someone my tale, as well. I used to be a factory worker. I was happy, I worked hard during the week and on weekends had a lady friend to keep me busy."

He shifts his gaze to me. "Then something happened," he says. "Somebody in my family was killed, assassinated. Not for anything they did, but because someone told untrue stories about this person. Falsehoods told to the wrong people will do that, will get a man killed. I had to avenge that death. That is how it began, Sarah."

I look at him quizzically.

"When people know you have killed a man," he explains, "they seek you out. They say please. Help me. You tell them you only committed this act out of vengeance, to avenge the murder of an innocent man. They say, '*Si señor, yo tambien!*' I want this man dead because he raped my wife. This man I want killed for trying to murder my grandfather.

"You will believe them," Romeo tells me. He leans close to me and his eyes stare into mine, searching. "You will believe them because you are green and angry. Still filled with heat in spite of your revenge. Looking for a place to put this anger. So you believe them because you *believe* them. Later, you believe them because it suits you to do so. Eventually, you don't believe them at all, not even the few who are not lying. You don't care. You travel and trade in bad people. These are all bad people. Why should you not line your pockets with their lives?"

He sits up straight, sips his tea. Shaking his head he says, "But you are not bad people. Nothing I can tell myself will make me believe this time. So now you know it all, *señorita*. Why I kill for money and why I'm not killing you. You know how it began, and how it continues."

I find I can't look at him. I gaze out over his head to the sky above him, now a stunning purple and red. "How will it end?"

Romeo's voice holds gentle laughter. "Someone will assassinate me."

"The Cabrera brothers?"

"Yes. Someone they hire. Today, tomorrow? These could be my last minutes to enjoy."

Now I do look at him. I shake my head, disbelieving. "Why would you do that? Why would you risk your life for me?"

He gazes at me pointedly.

I put my hands up, surrendering. "Just curious."

Romeo considers me, seems to make a decision.

"Many years ago, someone did me a favor. I have owed this favor for a long time, but I always was assured that God would tell me when the time had come to repay it." He nods in my direction. "It has come today."

We sit in silence for a long while and I ponder this strange man next to me, this man who has his own code and keeps strictly to it. He takes another drink from his tea then stretches out the way he did on the park bench, with his ankles crossed and his hands behind his head. His eyes are closed now, he appears asleep.

There is a small group of birds behind us. Tiny, nervous birds, chattering and flitting about, looking for crumbs. I take a piece of bread from the basket they brought us with our drinks, then twist my chair around so my back is to the table. I pull small pieces off the bread and watch the birds struggle with each other over the morsels. They are very fluffy, with bright orange beaks, and very bold, coming within inches of my fingers.

"Romeo?"

"Hmm?"

I lean way over, to try to get one of the little birds to eat from my hand. "Do you believe in heaven?"

Pop!

Crimson splashes bright against Romeo's white shirt. And everything stands still for a split second.

Instinct scrambles me from my chair. I crouch down behind the table, and from here I catch a glimpse of a man in jeans and a black T-shirt. He wears thick black gloves. He is not six feet from us, gun still raised. How did we not see him? Romeo, how?

The women at the table nearest ours scream. I'm thinking: *I'm next!* I leap from the table and shove the women out of my way, hurdle over the little white picket fence. My feet slap! slap! against the pavement. My breath goes ragged and my heart pounds in my ears. I peer over my shoulder. No one. I stop. Not smart maybe, but I do it anyway and run back the block I've come. Maybe he wasn't shot, maybe I made a mistake, maybe...

A crowd has gathered, hysterical. A woman is pointing down the alleyway and screaming "He went that way, he's there!"

I ease through the ring of people. No one stops me or seems to recognize that I just ran off. I look closely at my hit man-turned-guardian. His eyes are still closed.

"Romeo?"

No response. There is a hole in his chest and I see that the back of the chair is spattered with blood.

I put two fingers against his strong, lean neck. Nothing.

A tear runs down my face. For this monstrous man who spared my life, I am crying. One tear, then another.

Romeo is still smiling.

The distant whine of sirens pulls me from my reverie. If the cops take me in, I'm dead for sure. The Cabrera brothers will kill me on the way to the station house.

I jerk Romeo's Porsche keys from his belt loop and push back through the crowd again, my hand to my face. People ask me did I know him? Am I all right? I just nod. Once I break free from them, I cross Sunset and run again, all the way down La Cienega's steep hill, not stopping until I get to my street. I slow to a walk halfway up the block from my place. My chest and throat are burning, my calf muscles ache, I swear I'm on fire. But the farther I walk, the better I feel. Soon my breathing is normal, even though my throat still stings. My mouth is parched, and I am dreaming of a huge glass of cool water when I see Madeline's new yellow Beetle outside my building.

Fear crashes through me again. Only this time the fear is for someone else. I start running, but my body forbids it. Pain slams me harder, stomps most of the fear into a cold dread.

My front door is still open. Collapsed face down in my kitchen is my sister, who looks just like me. There is a small wound in her temple and just a trickle of blood. Quick and painless, like Romeo promised. And I understand now that he hadn't been guessing, he *knew*, knew they were coming for him and for me, knew that Madeline would be mistaken for me if I wasn't there.

Only Madeline didn't *do* anything. She didn't do anything! And who are these people to kill a girl for their mistakes anyway?

There is something new in me now, not the sadness I expected, but something ferocious. The rage and howl of the need for vengeance. Sure, I'm green like Romeo said, but I'm not stupid. I know it's easier to get a gun in Hollywood than it is to make a phone call. I know that there are advantages to people believing that you're dead. And I know a whole hell of a lot about chemistry, more than enough to kill somebody. Or three somebodies: the man who pulled the trigger and the brothers who hired him to do it.

I heave my stuffed duffel bag over my shoulder and make my way down the stairs and out to the black Porsche. *My* black Porsche.

Hollywood has been called many things—a lot of them unprintable. But the most accurate description is the one that postulates it is not so much a place as a state of mind. Sunset Boulevard runs through both. The intersection where Sunset meets its even more famous (or infamous) sister, Hollywood Boulevard, marks the site where once stood the towering walls of a Babylonian palace, erected by D.W. Griffith for his silent epic Intolerance. *The ability to take people off the streets and transform them into something they are not is the power that has fueled this area for nearly a century. With the right attitude—and the right costume—anyone can become anything in Hollywood.*

Even a killer...

TWO MULES FOR SISTER SARITA

By Kate Thornton

The smell of the place hit me as I opened the door. It was brightly lit, cluttered and cheerful, but all secondhand stores have that old-clothes smell.

"Welcome to A Star Is Born Again," the clerk said as I inched my way past a display of fifties halter dresses in Hawaiian prints. I had my eye on a pair of high-heeled turquoise mules I'd seen in the window a few days before, but I did a double take at the clerk's ensemble. It was tasteful and subdued, maybe the sort of outfit Sister Mary Carita at Immaculate Heart might have sported just before they dropped the habit requirement altogether, but it was still a nun's habit.

"Thank you," I murmured. A nun's habit is one of the more difficult drag looks to pull off properly, as you can't use makeup or rely on wigs or flashy clothes. I should know—I'm a fairly successful entertainer myself, a headliner at the Cage, although I was doing my shopping in my street clothes of jeans and a T-shirt. I never wear drag on the street.

I had wanted to check out the new shop on Sunset for some time. Resale shops come and go on that part of the boulevard, and if you don't make time to do them properly, you might miss something. In my business, I can't afford to pass up a good deal on a piece of vintage clothing in my size.

It was a little close in the shop, what with all the merchandise and several other customers. I spotted two guys giggling in a corner near a life-sized cutout of Elvis Presley. The tall one with purple hair and teeny-weeny pink sunglasses flipped through a stack of old movie magazines while the short, beefy one with the L.A. Raiders cap on backwards held up a couple of oversized brassieres. I hate that backwards cap thing.

"How much is this?" An older woman in several coats and a fur hat bawled in a loud Fairfax voice. She waved a ratty mink stole over her head. It was seventy-five degrees out and I had never seen a mink stole worn offstage.

I picked the mules out of the window display and slipped off a loafer to try one on. They were a wee bit tight, but I could make do. I turned them over and saw the price. Very reasonable. They would look great in my latest act at the Cage, a tribute to the sex kittens of the early sixties.

A hand shot out and grabbed the mules.

"Hey, lemme see those." The purple haired kid in the teeny-weeny sunglasses put his hairy paws on my mules. I mean really!

"Excuse me," I said, "but those are mine. Besides," I pointed out the obvious to him, "they wouldn't go with your look." I mean, he was a fashion disaster. Those gorgeous mules would look just ridiculous on him.

He released them and scowled at me. I hate confrontation, but those mules were worth one, and I was prepared to make a scene if I had to. If he was looking for dramatics, he came to the right girl, let me tell you.

"Jeez, leave 'im alone," Raiders Cap said. "Let's

get outta here before we start lookin' at dresses, for crissake!"

They left and I regained my composure by holding tight to my little mules and flipping through the gleaming racks. Of course, I found a stunning black taffeta. Regretfully, I put it back. Right size, wrong look. I need to stay focused when I shop or I'll end up with a bunch of stuff that just sits in the closet. I found a Marilyn dress, a white pleated halter knock-off, in perfect condition, but I knew what my shoulders would look like in it.

Then I saw what I was looking for, the perfect outfit. Well, the makings of a perfect outfit. They were the most delicious capri pants, glittery red, and just my size. I could see them with a plain white shirt knotted at the waist and those impossible turquoise mules. The right makeup and the big blond wig, and I could do "Kitten With a Whip." I checked the price tag and grinned.

I took my finds to the counter clerk whose nametag read "Sister Sarita." The doorbell jingled as another customer came in.

"Will that be all for you, sir?" the sister asked.

I nodded. "Do you have layaway?" I hadn't brought enough cash with me to do both the capris and the mules, and the sign on the register plainly read, "No Checks or Credit Cards."

"Sure, here, fill this out. And I'll need a ten dollar deposit."

I put my name and address on the form and laid a ten dollar bill across it as she rang up the purchase. She listed the items on the form, stuck my stuff into a paper bag from Trader Joe's, and stapled it closed with the form folded over the top. The bag went on a shelf behind the counter with a couple of other bags.

Sister Sarita smiled. "If you're looking for something special, I can keep an eye out for you." Sister Sarita had a breathy little girl's voice and a plain, homely face. Her glasses were of the utilitarian kind, and up close, she really did resemble a nun, a real one. But she'd never pass for Audrey Hepburn, that's for sure.

That night I tried out my Ann-Margret routine in a more subdued outfit, and let me tell you, it was terrific. I never got such an ovation from the crowd, and even that bitch Gordo who does the Liza turn had to admit it looked pretty good. I knew those mules and capris were going to be a big hit.

Next day I had an audition for a commercial and before you knew it, a week had gone by. I didn't get the part, but there was always another part on the horizon, and time flies when you're looking good. I love my work at the Cage, but I keep hoping for that big break, too.

It was one of those perfectly warm sunny days when the palm fronds wave and you wish you had a pool so you could sip a Cosmopolitan and ogle a pool boy or two. It was late afternoon when I went back to the resale shop. The door made that little jingle noise as I pushed it in to breathe the smell of used clothes. I gagged. There was another smell, a pungent, sour odor. I blinked as I started to make my way toward the counter.

The door jangled behind me and someone pushed in. "Hey," a raucous voice croaked, "what the hell stinks in here?"

I turned around. She was a tall woman, nearly my height, with a sun-browned wrinkly face, dyed black hair in a bouffant and too much fuchsia lipstick. From the looks of her clothes, she was a frequent shopper at A Star Is Born Again. I have to admit I coveted her polka-dot blouse and those fuchsia capris. I looked down—yes, there were fuchsia mules to complete the ensemble. "Hey," the woman said again, "what's goin' on here?" She pushed past me to the counter and shrieked. There was blood everywhere and broken shards of ceramic. The shelves behind the counter were empty. "Holy shit." She wheeled around to me. "Don't move, buster, not a muscle." She reached for the telephone without taking her eyes off me. I could see Sister Sarita's outflung hand on the floor in a pooling brownish stain.

The woman dialed 911. "Get over here pronto," she barked in her lapdog growl. "Someone's been murdered, and I got the guy right here." She gave the address and hung up.

"Hey, wait a minute," I said. "I just got here. She's been dead for a while, if that's what we smell."

"Yeah, maybe you have a point, sport." She scrunched up her nose. You could tell she'd been a good-looking woman before time, gravity, and cigarettes had taken their toll. "Only, I think we're smellin' the bowels, ya know? Shit! Dropped my keys."

She rooted around behind the counter for a second, her bracelets clicking together, swearing under her breath. When the wail of a siren broke the silence, she stood up and changed expressions. "I'm Tina Taylor," she said, obviously expecting me to recognize her name. She smiled and put out a liver-spotted hand with two-inch fuchsia nails.

I tried hard to think of where I had seen her. "Dennis Stone," I replied shaking her hand. I don't usually give out my stage name, Lady Darleena, to women I don't know. Not everyone understands the drag entertainment biz. "So, where do I know you from?"

She grinned. She must have been sixty if she was a day, and her skin had gone south along with her considerable bosom. "Maybe you remember me from *Bikini Beach Girls Go Hawaiian*," she said. "I was Tiffany in six of those pictures." She seemed to have forgotten the dead body at her feet.

"Oh, yeah." Tina Taylor had been the premier Gidget knock-off in the B beach movies of the early sixties. I would have killed for her old wardrobe. Then I looked over at Sister Sarita and shuddered. Maybe not.

Just then the door jingle-jangled and the cops arrived. Sister Sarita, whose real name turned out to be Bennie Shapiro according to the California driver's license in his wallet, was dead as a doornail, her head bashed in with a ceramic TV lamp in the shape of a pair of black leopards. The cops took preliminary statements and ushered us out onto the sidewalk. A forensics unit arrived and for about an hour the place swarmed, then an ambulance took Sister Sarita away. We were released, and Tina Taylor's Bakelite bangles rattled on her skinny wrist as she waved to me before sashaying away herself, click-clacking down Sunset.

I went back inside the store. All the cops were gone except for one plainclothes guy with a notebook. "Uh, excuse me," I said to him. "Uh, I had some stuff on layaway here, do you think..."

He squinted at me and scowled. I got that creepy feeling in the pit of my stomach, and I thought for a minute he was going to say or do something I'd regret. I run into guys like that sometimes, big macho types who just want to beat the crap out of you. I took a step backwards.

He was between me and the door and I didn't think there was a back way out. We were alone, so anything he did to me would be my word against that of an LAPD cop. I was close to fainting.

"Hey," he said, stepping closer, "aren't you Lady Darleena?"

I was too startled by the question to answer, so I just nodded. "Great show," he said with a grin. "Love that Ann-Margret thing. Where do you come up with those ideas?"

I sagged against the counter. "Uh, thanks. I, uh, I guess I get 'em from everywhere," I said lamely. Then I perked up. "Listen, Officer—"

"Detective," he corrected me. "Detective Art Gibford. Call me Art." He had a beautiful voice.

"Uh, Art, can I look for my stuff? I had things for the show on layaway here. I don't see any of the layaway stuff, and I just want to make sure it's still here."

"Where was it?"

"The layaway bags were on that shelf, up behind the counter there. Only I don't see any of them. There were five or six of them here last time I was in." The shelf was empty except for an assortment of tiny wire framed sunglasses in different colors.

He pointed to the floor, and I saw several bags torn and scattered and a couple more still intact. Mine wasn't there, but I saw the little receipt with my name on it on the shelf. The forensics team had already done their thing, so I didn't see any harm in picking it up. Then I spotted another piece of a receipt stuck to the bloodstained floor under the counter next to another pair of tiny sunglasses. It must have been under poor Sister Sarita. I picked it up, too.

"It's no use," I said, "my bag is gone."

Art nodded and wrote something in his notebook.

He had beautiful hands.

"You know, I've never been involved in anything like this before," I admitted.

Art sighed. "I see it all too often. A robbery gone bad and someone dead, it happens more than I want to think about."

"So you think this was a robbery?" I asked. "Then my bag is gone for good?" I tried to keep my voice from spiraling up into a squeal, but I was too distracted by the thought of those beautiful mules, and too aware of this gorgeous hunk of an officer standing ever so close to me.

"Probably. But we'll do all we can," he assured me. Detective Gibford put a consoling hand on my shoulder and then reached into his coat pocket for a business card. He wrote something on it and gave it to me. "Call me if you think of anything that could help." He smiled and gave my shoulder a squeeze. "Anything."

I glanced at the card where he had written a private phone number. I smiled back. I would try very hard to think of something.

I didn't have to work that night and spent the evening watching old movies, but not even *The Little Foxes* could get my mind off poor Sister Sarita. I might as well have been watching *The Nun's Story*.

I thought about Detective Gibford, too. I wanted to call him, but I wanted a better reason than just because I thought he was too gorgeous to be true. I dug out those receipts I had picked up and studied them. Damn, I had wanted those mules.

Then it hit me. The killing of Sister Sarita wasn't simply a random act. It was deliberate murder, and I now knew who had bashed in the nun's head with the TV lamp and why. And I had the perfect excuse to call Detective

Gibford.

Less than an hour later Art and I were seated in a booth at the Alibi. I showed him my receipt for the layaway, and then I showed him the other receipt, the one I had picked up from the bloodstained floor. "Someone else wanted those turquoise mules," I said.

His handsome face broke into a grin as the pieces of the puzzle fell into place. "Nice going." He reached for my hand and I felt the electricity buzz through me.

After bashing Sister Sarita over the head, the murderer had gone through the bags and taken not only my mules and capris, but the mules and capris from another layaway bag as well. It was the receipt from that bag—the murderer's own—that gave her away, since it listed her fuchsia mules, capris and Bakelite bracelets. Tina Taylor must have realized that receipt could be damning and came back to search for it, only I had already wandered into the shop. The halfhearted attempt to pin it on me was just desperation.

They tell me Tina Taylor was totally gaga when the cops arrived at her Sunset apartment. Dressed to kill in her *Beach Blanket* bikini, her hair in a teased flip, she batted her false eyelashes and tottered to the squad car in the fuchsia mules that doomed her.

But I had more important things to think about, like seeing Detective Art Gibford at the Cage at a table right up front, cheering me on. Gordo says he looks just like Roger Smith to my Ann-Margret.

I love show business.

The term "East Hollywood" has fallen out of use in recent years. The point where Sunset Boulevard passes the public television station—formerly a Poverty Row film studio from whence escaped the cheapest detective, crime and horror programmers of the 1940s—and makes a sharp bend to begin its due westerly course, has long since been absorbed into Hollywood proper. At one time, however, it was as recognizable an area as its more fashionable northern neighbor, Los Feliz, if far less likely to be frequented by the city's notable. For the city's notorious, however, any neighborhood is fair game...

NEITHER TARNISHED NOR AFRAID

By Gay Toltl Kinman

Wednesday, July 1, 1942. I'm walking a beat on Sunset where Hillhurst and Hollywood Boulevard collide and where you can wander off into Hollywood without even trying. Sunset weaves all the way from downtown, gets religion here then goes straight, loses it as soon as it hits the westside of Hollywood, gets drunk and meanders around until it ends up at the ocean.

I'm a cop—Officer Agnes Graham. Yeah, the same last name as the Assistant Chief. I'm not above pulling strings to get the job I want. Being 5'10" and big-boned helps. This is the only job I've ever wanted since Dad showed me his badge in its leather case. I must have been all of three years old.

If there wasn't a war on, I wouldn't be out here patrolling in LAPD uniform. The men who were cops are now overseas in a different kind of uniform, and they know exactly who their enemy is.

The brass at LAPD don't really want a woman in the center of any crime scene, but maybe they figured that here on Sunset I'd be out of trouble. What they didn't know was that I attract the stuff.

The partner I had was a big lout. Part of him drooped over his beltline. But he was likeable, and he didn't paw. So when he got shot instead of me, the brass were a little surprised. When I saved his life, their surprise turned to incredulity. Oh, gee, was he supposed to be protecting me? Guess I hadn't read that part of the script.

I decided to find the punk who shot my partner. When I did, the brass went beyond incredulity, if there's a word for that.

Glad as I was to be marching around in my uniform, I now wished I had another beat. The reason: a crazy lady who lived on Sunset. Mrs. Murgatroyd. Out of the blue, like somebody plugged her in, she started making calls, driving the dispatchers, the prowl car officers, the brass, and now me, crazy.

She kept seeing all kinds of crimes being committed. She'd call the police like a good citizen should. Only there wasn't any crime. Not even close.

The problem the brass had was that they couldn't ignore Mrs. Murgatroyd's calls. What if she really saw something and nobody came to investigate? Worse, what if someone important got hurt? Or even complained? The newspapers would have fun. The police department was always fodder for their print stables.

My presence on Sunset was supposed to solve all that. Yeah. Sure.

Like late yesterday afternoon, when I was on the beat, a prowl car swung by because Mrs. Murgatroyd had called in a burglary. What had I seen, they asked? I'd seen the guy across the street come home tired, pick up his newspaper and go into his house, probably looking forward to a nice evening of relaxation in his easy chair next to the radio.

Then I had the fun job of taking the "report" from Mrs. Murgatroyd. I imagined hearing the boys in the prowl car snickering all the way up Sunset. I'd feel the same way if I could drive off.

That's the way it had gone almost every day.

As I said, crazy.

So, here I am, walking my beat, thinking about a big glass of cold water with lots of ice, when an Olds pulls up and a guy gets out. Not bad-looking in spite of the fact that his face had seen a few fights. He carried himself well, with confidence.

"Officer."

"'Morning," I said. In spite of the heat, he was wearing a jacket one size too big—for a reason. But he wasn't Homicide. They all wore hats. I put my hand on my holstered gun.

He lit a cigarette, drew on it and waved the match out. "Gladys Murgatroyd live around here?"

I sized him up before saying anything. "Who are you?" Had trouble shown up already?

He held my gaze for a moment, then pulled his wallet out, the leather worn and shaped to his hip. He flipped it open, and I noted a leather cover over his ID. He handed me a pristine card.

Philip Marlowe
Private Investigator

"I've heard of you," I said. So now I'd finally met him. I put the card in my shirt pocket behind my notebook.

He gave me the impression he was thinking about which way I meant it, good or bad. He curled his upper lip over his top teeth as though checking to make sure they were smooth.

I eyed him again. Dad had talked about him more than once with respect, and he usually didn't take to P.I.s.

"There." I nodded to the big, shabby, pseudo-Victorian house across Sunset.

He squinted at it through a screen of smoke. "Some more icing, a few candles, and it'd be sagging." He turned and squinted at me. "Describe her."

"Why do you want to know?" I kept my voice hard and pleasant but not friendly.

"I'll trade information with you."

I considered him for a minute. What information did he have that I wanted? What did he want to know? My cop instincts were on alert. This was my patch on my watch and I didn't want anything to go wrong. Marlowe had a reputation for leaving a few bodies strewn around when he finished a job. If I went along with him at least I'd know what he was up to.

I decided to play the game. "Sixtyish, skinny, tall—"

"Taller than you?" Little crinkles in the corners of his eyes. Some day the smile might make it to his whole face.

"A few inches shorter."

He did that thing with his teeth again. "Go on. Hair color, eyes, etc."

"Short, frizzy, brown, but out of a bottle. I've never seen her without sunglasses so I can't tell you what color her eyes are. Face is sort of puffed up, considering she's thin."

He nodded. "Description fits."

"Of what?"

"Of a juror who's been threatened. Big mob trial downtown. My snitch says the mob guys know their boss is getting off and who on the jury is going to roll over." He glanced at the house again.

My brain was whirling a million miles a minute.

Somebody had given me a real assignment? That

goofy woman was on a jury?

None of it added up.

"Why her?"

"Old, alone—and the mob's got something on her."

"Mrs. Murgatroyd? The mob?" I shook my head. "She's crazy as a coot."

"Maybe. Maybe not." He said it as though he was mulling over the question, then he turned to me, a serious look in his eyes. "Always wondered how your father got so high up in the department when he was straight. I heard he saved somebody's life."

I nodded. The way my dad had told me the story, it was an accident and because of that he now had a *patrone*. He never told me what kind of accident. Maybe he was downplaying his heroism.

Maybe it was the truth.

"Guy's life he saved was Sonny Agostini," he said. "Doesn't hurt to have him on your side." A touch of sarcasm shaded his voice.

Being high in the department might be considered a payment from Agostini. My dad was straight, and as far as I knew, that's all there was to his relationship with the mobster.

"Your turn to trade a little information," I said. "Why do you want to know about Mrs. Murgatroyd?"

He dropped the cigarette on the sidewalk and stepped on it. "Thought maybe we could save her life."

"We? You and who else?"

"You. And that's two questions I've answered. You owe me one." He got into the Olds and drove off while I stood on the sidewalk sweating in my blues, not thinking nice thoughts about the man my father had spoken of so highly.

If Marlowe thought he was going to come in here and take over my patch, he was mistaken.

I quick-marched to the intersection where Hillhurst crosses and Hollywood Boulevard is born, and checked the newspaper rack. The headlines were all about the war—Egypt in trouble from Rommel, sixty thousand 18-to-20 year old men registered for the draft—and the Agostini murder trial.

Well, well. I didn't read any of the four rags in town, hearing enough lies on the job.

Picking up the *Los Angeles Times* I read:

Sonny Agostini's trial for the murder of Dewey Harcourt ended yesterday following final arguments by the prosecution and defense. The two-month case is now in the hands of the jury.

"We have proved beyond a shadow of a doubt that this man killed Mr. Harcourt," prosecutor William Ireland told the jurors. "His solid gold cigarette case bearing his initials and fingerprints was found under the victim's body. What more could anyone want in the way of direct evidence?"

Agostini has repeatedly denied the murder. "I didn't kill him," he testified. "My cigarette case was stolen from me that night."

Daniel Trifoli, Agostini's attorney, predicted that the jury would acquit his client, who allegedly has ties to organized crime. "The so-called evidence is flimsy and circumstantial," Trifoli said.

Two years ago, Agostini narrowly escaped going to trial after being accused of the torture slaying of Ricky Lamb in a case that shocked the nation.

See page 14.

Good thing I wasn't on the jury. I already knew how I'd vote.

Ironic that Dad had saved the guy's life and I'd been assigned to watch the juror who could save him again. Why me?

* * *

That night my phone rang while I was sprawled on my sofa dozing. I jumped. Reaching for the black receiver, my hand hovered in mid-air as the telephone rang again. It sure wasn't anybody calling me for a date. The only calls I usually got were wrong numbers, or the Watch Commander ordering me to return to duty.

"Hello?"

"Graham? Marlowe. Our gal's in trouble, you'd better get over here."

"I'll call Dispatch..." But he'd already hung up. Damn. I started to dial, then it hit me, and I laughed. After all the times Mrs. Murgatroyd had called the police, driving everyone crazy, I was going to make the call for her?

I placed the receiver back in the cradle, my hand still on it.

Thoughts skittered through my mind.

In trouble...how?

Surely, she'd call the police?

"Damn you, Marlowe."

I stood there, my hand still on the receiver.

To call Dispatch or not to call? Was it really a question?

Decide, Agnes.

Listen to your gut? Or do what the academy instructor taught in class?

Follow protocol if you want to be considered for promotion. Or else it's the women's jail. No choice there.

Seen enough vomit for one lifetime.

The guys can play cowboy but you can't, not if you want to be promoted. Even going after your partner's shooter didn't win you a boxful of brownie points.

Agnes, you're stalling. Marlowe or Dispatch?

You save the juror. Maybe. What are you going to say when they ask you why you didn't call it in?

What if you don't save her?

What does your gut say?

If anything went wrong, it would be because I'd messed up, not because I'd let someone else, like Marlowe, take control.

* * *

Hyperion to Sunset was about five minutes in my clattery Chevrolet. I spotted Marlowe's Olds and pulled in behind it. There wasn't much traffic on the street. Marlowe was in his car, I could tell from the stream of smoke coming out of the driver's window. I got in.

"Okay, sweetheart, this is what we're going to do."

For the "sweetheart" alone, I could have shot him in his manhood with my ankle gun. "Marlowe, every man I've ever met wants me to be his handmaiden. I haven't been so far, and I'm not going to start now."

He appraised me as if considering what species I was. "You're your father's daughter, all right. How about 'partner?'"

"We'll see."

He stared at the house, "Someone's in there. I'll check out back. You go to the front door. You'll have to figure out how to handle it. Get a look-see. Don't do anything, otherwise I'll be attending a double funeral and

I don't have enough money for all those flowers." He opened his door to get out.

"Wait a minute, Marlowe." I didn't move. There were some questions I wanted answers to before I took anything resembling an order from him. "Why did you call me?"

"I told you all that when I said you were your father's daughter. Number one, I need a police officer to be sure everything is on the up and up. Number two, I need someone who's not bent. Number three, someone who's good on the job." He was ticking these off on his fingers. "Number four, someone who's smart, and number five, someone who won't take any guff from anybody." Then he used his index finger to point at me.

He got out then leaned in the window. "Mrs. Murgatroyd's got a better chance of celebrating the Fourth of July if we're on the job. Maybe that's why your father got you this assignment. Coming, Graham?"

I sat there filtering through everything trying to decide what was the truth and what he'd said to get what he wanted.

Was he making it all up to get my cooperation? Was this assignment from my father to patrol Sunset in front of Mrs. Murgatroyd's house a chance to prove myself? Make the brass sit up and notice me as a real police officer? Or did the powers that be hope I'd fall on my face proving that women weren't fit to be police officers? And, in particular, this woman?

What did being involved with Marlowe have to do with all of this?

Lots of questions, no answers, same as I'd had back at my house. I got out of the car, following my gut instinct.

The night was still hot, but Mrs. Murgatroyd's

windows were all closed.

I pulled out a small notebook and a pen. Then dug out two one dollar bills and uncrinkled them. I knocked on the door, practicing my smile to see if I still had one.

"Mrs. Murgatroyd?" I called out and held up the two bills. "It's your neighbor from up the street. I'm collecting on your pledge for war bonds." I was trying so hard to sound sweet that my voice was almost in the falsetto range.

Would she recognize me without my cap and uniform? If so, what would she do? Sigh with relief? Say my name? Did she even know my name? Maybe she'd just say, "Oh, Officer?" Could I get my gun out in time?

Too late to think about that now.

The door opened a crack. Mrs. Murgatroyd in her sunglasses.

"Oh, Mrs. Murgatroyd, I'm here to pick up your pledge." I gave her my best expectant puppy-dog look, pretending not to see a figure though the crack where the door met the frame, or the shadow of a person in the far corner of her living room.

She croaked out that she would get her purse, her voice marinated in fear. Definitely not the woman who'd been giving me copious information for my reports of the crimes she'd seen. She didn't recognize me, probably wouldn't recognize her own mother. They obviously wanted her alive until after the trial, but scared enough to vote their way as in "not guilty." Alive she was and definitely scared.

I knew I was facing a soon-to-be dead woman. They couldn't let her live to tell how the "not guilty" vote came about. If she voted the other way...

I kept smiling brightly. A mitt on her arm

prevented her from moving and a moment later a dollar was in her hand. She stared at it like she'd sprouted a sixth finger, then slowly handed it over as though terrified to give it to me, terrified not to. I perkily thanked her. And dutifully made a notation in my notebook.

And then it hit me. No prowl cars around.

Why hadn't she called?

"Oh, Mrs. Murgatroyd, can I have a glass of water?"

She made gurgling sounds as though she'd been shot in the throat. The hand on her arm held her in place. "No, no, I can't."

The door slammed shut.

I bounced cheerfully down the steps, dropped my notebook and bent to pick it up while eying the base of the veranda.

Yep, a cut telephone line.

I jauntily went to the next house, the good neighbor doing good. I saw the shade on a side window of the Victorian lift up and a figure move.

Good, they were watching me do my duty to God and country.

At the next house, I went through my pitch, then loudly asked for a glass of water. I got a dollar and the water.

Drink that in, hit man.

On to the next house. I was now out of view as Sunset curved.

No more houses after that, just closed businesses. I walked back to Marlowe's car and got in. He appeared in a few minutes.

"How many?" he said.

"Two." I related what had happened.

"And there's two in the kitchen but they don't seem to be mobsters. Just guys playing with pencils and brushes and little colored bottles of something on the table."

"What kind of bottles?"

He told me what he saw. I whirled that around in my brain and told him about the cut line.

"No prowl cars around, and no night officer patrolling. Looks like it's just you and me." He moved his jaw around like he was swallowing the word "sweetheart," then he said, "Partner."

"Who are you working for?" I said.

He paused for a moment then plucked a dollar bill from my hand. "How about Mrs. Murgatroyd...as of now."

"Why are you doing this, Marlowe?"

"Full of questions, aren't you?" He gazed at the house so long that I didn't think he was going to say anything more.

"Let's say I believe in justice. Agostini's no friend of mine. I've got ribs that still ache in damp weather and a buddy who's planted and didn't die too prettily. Ricky Lamb." He drew on what was now just a lighted stub. "I want to make sure Agostini gets the death penalty all nice and legal-like. Nobody's been able to pin any murders on him and he's done plenty. Witnesses disappear or have a memory loss. Without his cigarette case as evidence, they never would have pegged him for this one."

I thought about justice for a moment.

"They'll make their move right after the verdict," Marlowe said. "We've got to be one jump ahead of them to save her."

"You have a plan?" I sure didn't, but I wasn't about to tell him that.

He took his time, lighting a new cigarette with his

old one.

"Nope. That's what partners are for. Think on it. See you in the morning."

* * *

The next morning when I arrived on the beat, I noticed the pile of butts outside the Olds, probably amounting to a pack and a half. Marlowe must have staked out the house all night.

He gave me a wave as he drove off and I started to patrol.

Almost immediately my eye was caught by Mrs. Murgatroyd in a colorful muumuu, wild hat and even larger than usual sunglasses—and a cane. She wasn't leaning on it, and she didn't give me the impression she was in pain as she made her way to the bus stop, ready for another day in court.

As I pondered the apparition, Marlowe returned with two cups of coffee.

"How'd you know I like it black?"

He lifted his cup in a toast, "Real cops drink it that way."

We stood there in the shade of the magnolia tree, drinking coffee as we brought each other up to date on Mrs. Murgatroyd.

Suddenly, he crushed his cup. "I've missed something. You said she took the bus? Did any car follow her?"

"Lots of cars around, but I didn't see anyone pull away from the curb or out of the driveway. There'll be guys at the courthouse," I said. "Why follow her?"

I thought about the cane, the hat and the

sunglasses—too Hollywood—and the stuff Marlowe had seen on the kitchen table.

"A double! That's what those guys in the kitchen were doing with pencils and bottles. Make-up artists and they did someone over." Why hadn't I thought of that before?

"An actress. She must have come in the back way from the alley," Marlowe said. "The cane goes with the disguise...a person's walk is distinctive. With the cane, who can tell? It'll change her height, too." He didn't appear too happy. "I should've had somebody watching the back." He crushed his cup even harder.

"She can't fool the other jurors. They've seen her every day, up close."

"If they got a good actress, she could pull it off. Probably wore a shapeless outfit and floppy hat?"

I nodded.

"And you said she always wears sunglasses? That conceals part of her face. All she has to do is pretend she's ill, a cold or something and that would explain the difference in her voice."

"The other jurors probably think she's weird anyhow. Maybe nobody's too friendly with her." I had a chilling thought. "That means they'll kill the double, too."

"Agostini has to be convicted. There's always somebody else he has to kill. It'll never stop, unless he's stopped." He studied the house again. "She's got to still be in there."

"What if we try to get her out?"

"Exactly where is she? Stashed in the basement? There's a shed out back. Dandy place to stick somebody. Lots of rats for company."

I shivered in the 80 degree temperature. "She

doesn't deserve this. She's a juror, somebody trying to do the right thing."

"Yeah, well, you know how fair life is. Give it a poke and it'll dump a Chrysler Building full of bricks on you."

"I'll take the place of the double."

"A double for the double? How far do you expect to get—the first step on the veranda? They'd have one through your heart and two in your brain before you could whimper. I still don't have enough money for the flowers."

"The cut telephone line! What about disguising yourself as a repairman?"

He rolled the cigarette around on his lips. "I like it. Let's work out a plan."

So we did.

* * *

The overalls fit perfectly over my uniform. Marlowe also brought me a hat and wig and glasses. Shades of Mrs. Murgatroyd. And he drove a telephone company truck. I didn't ask where he got it, or how.

We made a great show of inspecting the lines. I went next door first and into the backyard, checking it out and making notations on my clipboard. Marlowe headed for the Victorian's backyard with a wheel of black wire and began stringing it out. While he was doing that I knocked on the front door and then heard sounds and mutterings inside, but no one answered. I hummed, checked my clipboard and knocked again. Still nothing. I clomped off the veranda, viewed the house, made notes. Then made a great show of finding the cut wire.

"Nobody's home. But I found a problem," I

shouted in bass, so they wouldn't recognize my voice from last night. "Cut line. Probably kids."

He yelled back. "We can fix it. Get the ladder, partner."

I headed back to the truck.

Partner. Get the ladder. I could carry it, but he'd be lucky I didn't drop it on him.

I slammed the ladder against the building. We shouted back and forth. Marlowe let out all the wire, then went back to the truck for two more reels, which we took next door. We set them on the ground and then I made a show of pointing to my watch, pantomiming drinking a cup of coffee. We climbed into the truck, sped off, then sneaked back to watch. We weren't disappointed.

Two guys ran out and around, peering at the wire and the ladder like we'd left scavenger hunt notes on everything. They kept checking out the windows in the front of the house and the one at the side.

"Bet she's in that front bedroom," I said.

Marlowe grunted.

One of the guys drove off in a Buick parked at the curb.

We went back, made a lot of noise again, me banging on the door, Marlowe thumping the ladder against the building on his way to the back of the house.

This time one of the guys opened the door, madder than a momma moose. "What the hell is going on?"

"We're replacing lines, sir," I said cheerfully. "Yours got cut. We'll have you back in service in no time."

"I don't want telephone service. If I did, I'd have asked for it. I want peace and quiet. Get off my property."

He didn't see Marlowe come up behind him, but I

could tell he felt the gun to his back because he froze, his eyes darting around like black marbles. He started to move his hands up as I drew my gun and pushed through the doorway.

Mrs. Murgatroyd was tied up in her bed. Marlowe pulled the truck into the driveway and we bundled her into it. The guy we sort of tossed in the back, trussed up like a Sunday dinner chicken.

* * *

Mrs. Murgatroyd turned out not to be so crazy after all. She told us she figured if there were a lot of cops around, the mob wouldn't try to do anything to her. She also hoped that if everyone thought she was crazy, they'd take her off the jury. She didn't have luck in either category.

* * *

"Why are you so sure Agostini killed Ricky Lamb?" I said afterwards. We were sitting in the truck, back at my beat on Sunset.

"Over two years ago as Lamb lay dying, Agostini bent over him, the cigarette case fell on the floor and Lamb rolled over it. Agostini left, probably realized he didn't have it, figured out what happened, went back and got it. Gave Lamb another kick in the head."

I stared at him. "How do you know all this?"

"I found the body—and the cleaning lady who saw everything."

"The cleaning lady. Then why—"

"Why didn't she testify? She decided changing the

color of her hair, losing a few pounds and moving would extend her lifeline." He glanced at the old Victorian.

I looked also. "Mrs. Murgatroyd? That's what you meant when you said the mob had something on her? That she'd seen the murder?"

Marlowe nodded.

"When they found her why didn't they just kill her?"

He studied his cigarette. He hadn't lit it yet. Maybe he was thinking about giving them up. "The way I see it is that they figured she was worth more alive than dead."

"Being a juror?"

"Being a juror they can control. They promise not to kill her in return for her vote. She's not going to talk, and they don't have to worry about the taint of scandal about jury tampering. She thinks if she votes right, they won't kill her."

"And we know whichever way she votes she's dead."

Marlowe lit up sending a stream of smoke downward.

"It's really odd that the same thing happened twice," I said, trying to work everything out. "Agostini losing his cigarette case twice next to a body? Only the second time he doesn't go back to get it?"

Marlowe stuck the cigarette between his teeth. "Yeah, odd, isn't it."

We stared at each other for a long moment.

Was he wondering how straight a cop I was? Straight enough to report our conversation? Bent enough not to?

But he already knew the answer to that one. Maybe

it had something to do with justice.

The next day I was walking my beat on Sunset when Marlowe showed up with coffee.

"Happy Fourth," I said. This time I lifted my cup in a toast. "Mrs. Murgatroyd is still alive, and maybe even celebrating."

"Thanks to you. I'm making sure the brass gives you full credit for this." Marlowe studied the slightly curved cigarette he'd just shaken out of crushed pack as though embarrassed to meet me eye to eye.

For a moment, I was speechless, then I stuck out my hand and we shook. "Thanks, partner," I said.

We just stood there. Then I said, "How did Mrs. Murgatroyd get on the jury in the first place?"

He gave me half a grin. One of these days, I might get the full one. "What would you do if a marshal came to your door and told you to appear for jury service?"

"A marshal? They don't have time to do that."

"The mob can arrange anything," Marlowe said. "Even her summons. What better way to control the jury than have someone who isn't going to complain. And who's going to vote the way they want."

"It would have been a smart move for them if it had worked out."

"You're several answers ahead in our information trade, but I'll call it even if you answer this one. You said you heard about me—what did you hear?" he said keeping his eyes on mine.

"Dad said you were a tough guy—neither tarnished, nor afraid."

He nodded, concentrated for a few moments on lighting his cigarette and fixed his eyes on me. "Don't believe everything you hear." Then he got into the Olds and waved as he drove up Sunset.

I watched the man who called himself Marlowe moving away. "Nah," I said out loud. "Marlowe'd never plant evidence—not even in the name of justice. The guy has to be someone else."

No one answered me.

We're traveling through the center of Hollywood now on a street as straight as the path of an arrow. Here Sunset and Hollywood Boulevards run perfectly parallel, like twin rails of an enormous train track. Countless people have bought tickets for this particular railway, boarding anywhere in the world there are dreams, hoping to pull into Fame and Fortune Station at the other end. Some have made it. Many more were transferred onto another line, the one leading to South Disappointment. But for some unfortunate souls, the journey was suddenly cut short before either destination was in view.

Love it or hate it, one thing has to be admitted: Hollywood has never had a shortage of dreamers.

Or victims...

AN OPEN AND SHUT CASE

by Mae Woods

Donna Driscoll pushed her chair back from the Avid as the editor switched on the lights. The production team of *Hollywood Homicide* squeezed around her in the edit bay, waiting for her comments. She wanted to scream, *It's drivel.*

Instead, Donna soldiered on, mustering up constructive guidance. "This piece is a bit too hocus-pocus for us, guys," she began carefully. "Maybe the ghost of Paul Bern *did* warn Sharon Tate not to go to Cielo Drive, but she didn't listen to him. Our show should focus on her murder, not the speculation of parapsychologists." She turned to the editor. "Amy, could you pull up all the news footage? We can try portions of the interviews as voice-over, get rid of some of the talking heads before Hal sees it."

"Hal's already seen it," Amy said quietly. "He approved it. It airs next week."

Donna bit back her anger as she pounded down the hall to confront Hal Jacobs. She found the short, balding man hunched over a production budget. He looked like a mild-mannered accountant, not a high-energy producer who had breezed in from Chicago, set up a production company and sold two reality series in one week.

"Hal, is something going on I need to know? Did

a memo go out saying we're streamlining production, and the staff doesn't need to work with the supervising producer anymore? I didn't get a copy of the memo, but I sure got the message."

He looked confused. "What's this about?"

"I've just been giving notes on a piece you apparently already put to bed. What's worse, everybody seemed to know it but me."

Hal looked surprised by her bitterness and spoke in a placating tone. "Craig thought there might be a legal issue, so he asked me to look at it before it was finished. I saw it this morning. There wasn't a legal problem. I liked what I saw, so I approved it. Nobody went behind your back. Don't make a big deal about it."

Donna stared at Hal. He looked genuinely sincere. She paused.

"Just keep me informed. Okay?" she said coolly.

"No problem."

Hal probably would have overruled her on the segment anyway, Donna realized. He liked tabloid stories, and he had the final say. She headed to her office. She'd spent most of the day finalizing end credits and clearances. No wonder she was irritable. She was the senior writer and supervising producer, but she had to do tasks usually handled by the production coordinator because the show was short-staffed. She wanted to concentrate on the stories. Donna had worked as a newspaperwoman for six years, then as a TV reporter for another three before joining Hal. He hired her to host the initial *Hollywood Homicide* promo. She was thirty-four, blond, pretty, articulate and poised on camera. She was also smart enough to know she'd have a longer career behind the camera than in front of it. She'd convinced Hal to put her on the writing staff and had risen to producer/writer the next season.

She stared at the clock. At six, it would give her permission to head across the street to Cat & Fiddle for a drink. Later, she could return to finish her work without the jangle of phones.

She felt a rush of freedom as she stepped inside the lively pub.

"Hey, Pete." Donna slipped onto a barstool.

"Miz Driscoll. What'll it be?" He smiled.

"Harp."

"Great beer, and an invitation to vent. I like that in a beverage."

"You don't want to hear me vent. It would shatter all your Waterford." Donna laughed as Pete foamed out a lager. She glanced up at the TV. "CNN? We at war?"

He tipped his head toward a booth in the corner. A group of young people were laughing and making their way through a pitcher of beer.

"So, the news puppies from up the block are logging some 'happy hour' time. I've been coming here for years and have yet to see channel 23—"

Pete pressed the remote, bringing forth a burst of cheesy music and a close shot of a termite. "Your channel doesn't exactly liven up the room. 'Cept when *Hollywood Homicide* is on, of course."

"Very politic. And I'll take it as a compliment. Thank you. Try the local news. That should be good for a laugh."

Pete switched the channel to an intense young reporter standing in front of a stretch of yellow tape. Behind him was leafy foliage with the outline of a bridge peeking through the green.

Donna perked up. "That's Lake Hollywood."

She watched intently as the newsman reported a murder in a dark, somber tone. "The body of a young woman was found by hikers early this morning. Jennifer Crane, twenty-five, a model and aspiring actress, was strangled..." A photo of the victim filled the screen. She was blond and pretty with an engaging smile. She looked like a high school cheerleader, not a glamour girl. "...She was described by friends as a fitness buff who often jogged at Lake Hollywood Reservoir..."

Donna's eyes were riveted to the screen. Pete glanced at her with concern. "Hey, do you know her?"

"Nope. But there's something about this case— "

"Oh, it's a *case* to you. Not a dead girl. A case. Some poor dumb broad gets herself killed, and you light up like your team won the playoff—"

"'Poor dumb broad?' Now who's being callous?" She stood, fishing money out of a deep, black canvas handbag. She left three dollars on the bar and headed to the door.

"Hey, no offense," he called after her.

Donna stood at the curb, looking across at the Manufacturers Bank building. Once it had attracted stellar talent agencies and show biz companies. Those had been glorious days for this stretch of Sunset Boulevard. She could imagine Errol Flynn pumping iron at Hollywood Athletic Club, Caroline Leonetti models bouncing up the stairs to her agency, Frank Sinatra fans causing traffic jams outside Wallach's Music City. Now the high rise at 6565 anchored a block of dingy buildings and fast food stops. She headed down the street to cross at the signal.

Donna stopped to admire the Church of the Blessed Sacrament, glowing in the rosy haze of the setting sun. It made her think of Christmas, and she wondered where she'd be in December. Probably not here. She knew *Hollywood Homicide* had run its course. It had been easy to fill the first two years with juicy material. The third year had been harder. Now they were on year four, struggling to find fresh crime stories. Some of the new episodes weren't even about Hollywood. This week Hal had asked the interns to research circus murders for a "Death Under the Big Top" segment. Donna fervently hoped there hadn't been any, though she knew the young go-getters would find some tale of a trainer stomped by a berserk elephant or a midget clown-turned-snack in the jaws of a hungry lion.

Donna walked past her building to the parking structure. She wasn't going back to the office tonight. She would go home and start work on pitch ideas she could take to the networks. It was time to create her own show. Something solid. Investigative reporting, like she'd done before she got sidetracked by working for Hal.

She noted with satisfaction her name on her parking stall, one of the key evidences of success. She glanced at her watch. Seven-fifteen, but it was still daylight. The jogging path around Lake Hollywood Reservoir might be open. A brisk walk would sharpen her mind.

When she reached the reservoir, the entrance was chained shut. Donna could see through the trees to the bridge. She realized this was the spot where the TV reporter had stood. She walked over to a trash can. Wads of yellow tape lined the bottom. A bit of cardboard caught her eye. She fished out an empty film box. It was probably the police photographer's, but it reminded her the dead girl was a model. Maybe Jennifer Crane hadn't been jogging. Maybe she'd been up there on a photo shoot.

Donna stepped off the pavement into the brush. Patches of matted down weeds trailed into the heavily wooded area. A gust of damp air sent shivers down her bare arms.

"Hey!"

The voice jarred her. She spun around.

A county worker in an orange vest stood at the gate. "You looking for something? Park's closed."

"Just leaving." She walked over to him. "Terrible about that girl. Did the cops find anything?"

"Don't know. They just towed her car." He gestured to a spot by the edge of the road. The Hollywood cityscape sparked in the background. Nice photo, Donna thought.

As she navigated the winding road down Holly Drive to Cahuenga, she wondered why the death of Jennifer Crane nagged at her. There was something familiar about it. Maybe she'd covered a story like it in her early days as a reporter.

As soon as she got home, Donna logged onto her computer and opened Nexis-Lexis. What words might turn up a link? She typed in: *murder + strangle + model.* There were hundreds of hits. She added "Hollywood" and "blond" to the search box. That eliminated many entries, but there was still a lot of material to wade through. Then she found it: An *L.A. Times* article about the murder of Monica Pallin, a blond Hollywood model. Her body had been discovered in her sports car on Mulholland Drive in August 1994. Like Jennifer Crane, she'd been strangled. Donna followed the links to more articles and learned that Monica's ex-boyfriend and a photographer had both been suspects in the early stages of the investigation. But the fingerprints of a Hector Rios had been found on the car. He'd been charged with the murder and found guilty.

Donna wanted to know more. She jotted down

dates and names. She'd need the court transcript of the trial. *Hollywood Homicide* ordered many and had an account at the L.A. County Courthouse. Donna would send an office intern to pick it up in the morning. No, she would get it herself. She wasn't going to discuss this case with anyone. Her intuition told her there was a dramatic crime piece here. If she told Hal, he'd insist on playing up the sexy model angle. She wasn't going to do that. She'd develop it as a police story, linking the old case to the current murder headlines. In fact, *that* was a great premise for a TV series. She chortled at the thought of Hal unwittingly financing a piece she would later take to the network as the concept for a Donna Driscoll independent production.

At the downtown courthouse the next morning, Donna filled out a request for the trial transcript and paid the copying fee in cash. Thirty minutes later she was home at the kitchen table with a steaming mug of coffee, carefully underlining key information.

Hector Rios had no prior criminal record. He was twenty-two. He'd worked at Prestige Car Wash on La Cienaga. On the morning of August 10, he went to Monica Pallin's apartment on Larrabee to pick up her Corvette. He drove the car to Prestige for a hand wash and detailing then returned it at 1:30 pm. When he knocked on the door, he noticed it wasn't pulled shut. He opened it. Monica was naked, just leaving the shower. She was so angry that she phoned his supervisor to complain, and Rios got fired. Two days later Monica was murdered. Rios claimed he was with his girlfriend at the time of the crime. There was no testimony from her at the trial.

Hector Rios had been given a new address for the next twenty years: Corcoran State Prison. Donna wished it weren't Corcoran. It was a scorching, three-hour drive to the prison, dodging 18-wheelers on Highway 99. She'd been there on interviews before and had spent more time on the road than in the visiting room.

Donna noted the name of the arresting officer: Det. Michael Maguire, Hollywood Precinct. He and his partner Lewis Overbee had both appeared in court. She phoned the Hollywood police station and asked for Sgt. Bill Zarsky. He had recently helped her put together a piece on the murder of actor Sal Mineo.

"Hey, Bill, it's Donna Driscoll—"

"Is this the call I've been waiting for? You finally gonna put me on TV?"

"Maybe if you do something special—like solve a crime."

"Very funny. So, what can I do for you?" Zarsky asked.

"I'm researching an old murder case. Monica Pallin. Detectives involved were Michael Maguire and Lewis Overbee."

"Overbee died a couple of years back. Maguire's retired."

"Know how I can reach him?"

"Nope. David Sim was his last partner. I can ask him to call you, but I don't know that he will. He's starting a press conference right now. He's lead detective on a real hot one, the Jennifer Crane investi—"

"That's okay," she broke in. "I'll try him tomorrow. Thanks, Bill."

Donna had no intention of waiting until tomorrow. She raced over to the Wilcox Station, but when she got there, the press session was wrapping up. It must have been a brief status report. She stepped in the path of

Detective Sim as he left the conference room.

"Detective Sim, there are a lot of similarities between Jennifer Crane and Monica Pallin, that model who was killed in 1994," Donna began. "She was on a photo shoot up in the hills. She was blond. Both were strangled— "

"Pallin's killer is in jail," he interrupted. "And what makes you think Jennifer Crane was on a photo shoot? She was wearing a jogging outfit."

"It's worth looking into."

"We're checking out every lead. You'll have to excuse me. I've got work to do." He walked briskly up the hall.

Donna fell in step behind him. "Can you tell me how to reach Michael Maguire?"

He stopped and turned around. "Maguire?...You're not here for the press conference, are you?"

"I'm doing a TV piece about Monica Pallin for *Hollywood Homicide*. I'm Donna Driscoll," she said, handing him a business card. "I've been researching old cases set in Hollywood, and I was struck by the strong similarity between Monica Pallin's murder and Jennifer Crane's."

"That would make your show more newsworthy, of course," he commented with a wry smile.

"Of course. But our audience tunes in to revisit old crimes. They get today's headlines on the local news. I'd like to talk to anyone who worked on the Pallin case. You seem to remember it."

"I wasn't involved in it. I worked vice then."

"Can you give me Michael Maguire's phone number?"

"I'll phone Mack and ask him to call you. That's

really all I can do for you."

* * *

As soon as Donna left, Sim headed to the file room to pull the records of the Pallin case. Inside a bulky file, he found a composite glossy of Monica in casual garb, in eveningwear, and in a swimsuit. Sim turned it over. Gower Photos was stamped on the back. He fished out the police reports.

Back at his desk, Sim pored through his file on Jennifer Crane. Her head shot bore the Gower Photos' logo. He quickly sorted through the rest of the Pallin paperwork. He saw that William Reedy, the photographer at Gower, had been a suspect, but had been cleared. Sim walked across the room to another detective, handed him the photograph. "We need to talk to William Reedy at Gower Photo, see how well he knew Jennifer Crane. I'm fielding media calls now. Could you bring him into the box?"

Next, Sim phoned Maguire and asked him to stop by.

When Maguire arrived twenty minutes later, Sim stood and gave his beefy ex-partner a bear hug. Maguire wore a brown sport coat, and his hair, graying at the temples, was cut short. He looked exactly like all the other cops in the station.

"How's the life of leisure?" Sim asked.

"Great. But putting a kid through college on a pension is seriously eating into my golf fund."

"Maybe you ought to switch to aerobics, get one of those tight little Spandex outfits, hang out at a westside gym with the rich and buff."

"Tried that. Met all these gorgeous women. They were calling me every night. Cynthia got upset." Maguire grinned. "So, what's up?"

"I just had a visit from a producer at *Hollywood Homicide.*" Sim handed him Donna's card. "She's planning to do something on the Monica Pallin case. Wants to talk to you."

"Yeah? What do you think?" Maguire asked.

"Well, I'd talk to her if I were you." Sim stretched back in his chair. "I think it's better to be cooperative, find out what she's doing, make sure we're not gonna get dragged through mud on national TV."

Sim's gaze moved to the doorway as a detective entered with a slim, middle-aged man wearing a gray T-shirt and black Levis.

Maguire turned. "I recognize that guy. Why's he here?"

"I had him brought in. He's a photographer who knew Jennifer Crane. William Reedy, one of your suspects in the Pallin case. Donna Driscoll spotted a possible link between the two murders."

"I checked him out. He was clean."

"I knew it was probably nothing. The guy's a photographer so he meets lots of models, but I figured... Well, thanks for stopping by. Good seeing you." Sim stood, gathering together his papers.

Maguire stopped him. "Dave, have you got my reports there? Could I have a look? I'd like to bone up on the case before I talk to the TV people."

"Sure. Just leave everything on my desk when you're done."

Sim headed to the interview room. Maguire walked around behind the desk. He sank into Sim's chair and opened the file, whistling softly as he picked up a pencil and note pad.

When he finished reading, he gazed at the wall, troubled. The parallels between Pallin and Crane were clear. Had they nailed the wrong man? Maguire and Overbee had both thought Hector Rios was guilty. He'd been sullen and uncooperative throughout the investigation. William Reedy had breezed through his interview. Maguire remembered the photographer had an alibi, but it wasn't in the file. Now Overbee was gone. If there was a police inquiry, Maguire would face it alone. Twenty years of illustrious service would mean nothing if they ruled he'd been purposely negligent. They'd never do that, he reassured himself. He hadn't done anything worse than other cops. Only he'd be more visible if that TV show stirred up the case and Rios filed an appeal. Maguire drummed his fingers on the desk, thinking. He'd find a way out of this. He always did.

* * *

Maguire sat in his car across the street from Gower Photos. He hunkered down as a police car dropped William Reedy at the corner of Selma. The building, a blue stucco house that had been turned into a studio, was seedier than he remembered. The exterior paint was peeling. The beveled glass front door was protected by a white security gate. Clearly, the neighborhood—and the starlet photo business—had fallen into decline.

Ten minutes later Maguire rang the buzzer and watched Reedy come from the back room to press the door release.

"Do you remember me?" Maguire asked.

"You bet. If you're planning to haul me back to the station, I'm calling my lawyer. I just wasted two hours there. This is harassment, " Reedy fumed. "I've got work to do."

"Relax. We're not going anywhere. There was something my partner forgot to ask you. Do you know a woman named Donna Driscoll?"

Reedy's face was blank. "No."

"She works for the TV show *Hollywood Homicide.*"

"Don't know her."

"Then you don't know any reason she'd want to finger you for murder?"

Reedy snapped to attention. "What do you mean?"

"I'm wondering why she'd put you in a tough spot with the cops when there's no evidence against you." Maguire pressed. "Maybe there's something in it for her."

Reedy looked perplexed. He spoke slowly, "I never met her."

"Okay, that's all. For now."

* * *

Maguire whistled as he walked down the hall to the *Hollywood Homicide* suite. After the receptionist announced him, Donna ushered him into her cluttered office. "This is a surprise, Detective Maguire—"

"Call me Mack. I'm retired now. Thought it would be better to meet than talk on the phone. I understand you're doing something about Monica Pallin's murder on your show."

"Well, I'm just at the research stage—"

Maguire interrupted, "Do we need to stay here?

Maybe we could go for a drink, be a little more relaxed? That's one of the benefits of being retired. I can drink on the job, because there is no job. In fact, it may be the only benefit," he added with a quick grin.

"Sure. There's a good place right across the street." She scooped up a file folder and slipped it into her large canvas bag.

As they approached the Cat & Fiddle, Donna remarked, "From your comment about retirement, it sounds like you miss police work."

"Not the work. I made my twenty years, but the stress is—*was*—tough. I do miss the guys. My friends are still working, so there's no one to play with," he joked, opening the door to the restaurant.

They settled into a booth and ordered drinks. Donna pulled out her notes. "I read the transcript of the trial. There didn't seem to be any solid evidence against Hector Rios."

"His prints were on the car," Maguire interjected.

"But he'd polished it at the car wash where he worked."

"The *jury* saw that as solid evidence."

"Any idea why Rios didn't take the stand?"

"Maybe 'cause of the language thing. The guy could barely speak English." He drained his Jack Daniel's and gestured to the waitress for a refill. "Maybe the defense attorney advised against it. He looked like a hood."

"He didn't have a record though."

"True. But he failed the polygraph. That's not in the court record."

"Well, it couldn't be, could it? It's not admissible."

"Right. But it sure helped convince me," Maguire

said.

"Did you give him the lie detector test in Spanish?"

He paused. "No, that wasn't the procedure then. Now, we'd have to."

Donna wanted to take notes, but she couldn't reveal that he'd said something she planned to use in the on-camera interview. She quickly asked another question then made a small note.

"What do you remember about Monica Pallin?"

"Sexy girl, probably a little loose, like all those ladies who call themselves models."

"Wasn't she really a model? Isn't that how she made her living?"

"Yeah, I believe it was," he admitted, grudgingly.

She restrained her pen, wondering if Maguire figured Monica had deserved what she got. Donna was definitely going to lure him into this territory on-camera. She hid her thoughts behind an innocent smile.

Maguire smiled back. "Guess I was more focused on getting Rios off the street than I was on the victim."

"Did you talk to his girlfriend? Rios said she was with him at the time of the murder."

"Couldn't find her. She was here illegally. She got deported."

"Deported? Right after he was arrested? That seems odd."

"Happens all the time."

"Well, did you try to find her in Mexico—*was* it Mexico?" Donna probed.

"Mexicali. Right on the border. We contacted the police there, but they didn't find her." He leaned in closer. "My theory? She didn't want to be found. She knew he was the killer."

Donna's voice was even, conversational, "But wouldn't it have helped your investigation to find her—"

"Didn't need her. We *had* him. O-A-S, open and shut. You know, we didn't get the credit we deserved on that one. The investigation dragged on for months, and the goddamned *Times* kept it in the headlines, putting the pressure on us. It took us a little time to get it all sewed up. When we did, it was air-tight."

He leaned in conspiratorially. "Truth is, the cops always win in the end. Very few criminals get away with murder. You know why? Because we know exactly how they think."

"OAS..." Donna repeated.

Maguire drained his glass. "So, you're not sure about doing this story?"

"What?" she asked, surprised. Donna could barely wait to get home to write up her impressions of this meeting. It was going to be a fabulous story. She'd have to stay in Maguire's good graces and play along. She'd have to be sure he didn't sense the interview might make him look like a cop with an "attitude problem" on national television.

"At your office, earlier, you said you weren't sure about it."

"Oh, well, we don't like to commit until we complete the research," she explained.

He nodded. "Is this it, then? Or will I have to talk to anyone else?"

"No. I work alone. I'll set up interview time at the studio and call you."

* * *

It was dark when they approached the parking structure behind 6565. A milky beam from a street lamp dimly illuminated the entrance. The attendant's kiosk was shuttered. Maguire noticed that the light above it had been smashed. He steered Donna around the bits of shattered glass on the pavement. They said goodnight at her car, and he headed toward the street.

As Donna fumbled for her keys, Maguire moved into a dark corner. He stopped and leaned against the wall, watching her.

A shadowy figure crept out from behind the kiosk. Donna's head was down, looking in her handbag. Suddenly, she lurched backward, a nylon cord pulled taut against her neck. She dropped her bag and struggled to grab the cord. The man yanked her toward him.

Pressed against the wall, Maguire watched. Silent. Waiting.

Donna gasped. The cord pulled tighter. Tighter. The man's face grew red and contorted. Then, he relaxed his grip, and she slumped to the ground.

Maguire leaped out, revolver leveled. The noise of the first blast snapped Reedy's head around. He raised his hands in surprise and surrender.

Maguire powered forward, firing again and again. Reedy fell, blood seeping from his chest. Maguire approached the two bodies. He balanced his feet in an awkward spread to avoid stepping in the wet, red pool. He leaned over and checked each for the trace of a pulse. When he was certain both were dead, he carefully lifted the file folder out of Donna's bag. He'd toss that in the dumpster across the street while he waited for the boys.

He tapped out the familiar number on his cell phone. Sim was on call tonight. It would be easy to explain what had happened, how he'd heard a cry and rushed back to help Donna Driscoll. Too late. The cops would tie William Reedy to the Lake Hollywood slaying and close the book on it. Donna was his second victim. An open and shut case. After Sim completed the paperwork, they could grab a burger at Tommy's. Just like old times.

As we approach the corridor to the westside, Sunset Boulevard dips southwesterly and becomes curvy again. We are about to enter the fabled Sunset Strip, so called because its one-and-three-quarter mile length originally fell outside of the incorporated area of the city—and the city's rules. A one-time haven for speakeasies, gambling joints and nightclubs, the Strip has been a playground for the rich, the famous and the criminal set since the 1920s. Today the Strip is the place of modern high-rise hotels and office buildings, pricey boutiques and trendy eateries. What have not been lost, though, are the passions that can still course through the people who frequent the strip, dangerous passions that can burst forth at the strangest of times...

LOVE ON SUNSET BOULEVARD

By Linda O. Johnston

Tonight. It would happen tonight, Barbara was certain of it.

She stood alone in the swank and shimmering lobby of the Sunset Majestic Square, the extravagant hotel that stuck its nose high into the smoggy air not far from where Sunset curled into the wide streets of Beverly Hills.

Milo would meet her here as soon as his meeting was over. Dear, adorable Milo, a dot-com guru of the highest magnitude—whose business sense, along with his intelligence and wisdom, had allowed his company to weather the recent dot-com shakeouts and come out far above the rest.

Wonderful, wealthy Milo...

"We want room seven sixty-five tonight," she told the clerk at the reception desk.

The old geezer with the face of a camel was dressed like a royal Beefeater outside the Tower of London. His nametag I.D.'d him as Randolph. He had been here before when they had checked in. Barbara wondered if he made his home right there, behind the gleaming granite-topped desk.

"Room seven sixty-five? Certainly, Ms. Molows," he intoned stiffly, formally, deferentially. "We have it reserved for you. As usual."

He exaggerated, but so what? They had only stayed in the SunMaj three nights before, each time to celebrate something special.

Tonight would be the most special of all. Milo was going to pop the question. At long last. Barbara was certain of it.

"Thank you, Randolph." She accepted the plastic card key but eschewed the services of the bell captain. She was, after all, a thoroughly independent woman.

Still, the idea of Milo's proposing made her feel all feminine and squishy inside as she picked up her valise and took the elegantly appointed elevator to the seventh floor.

She was a woman who thought for herself. Pragmatically, she deferred to her bosses in her real estate office, and was cordial to customers. But she bent over for no one.

She could have proposed marriage to Milo, and long before this. But Milo was the sweetest, most old-fashioned of men. He held open doors. Walked along the curb as they strolled the streets hand in hand. Spouted the dearest, corniest, and most irritating expressions about relationships and love.

She loved him. He loved her. It was as simple as that.

And so, she would allow him the pleasure of getting down on one knee and asking her to become his wife.

The room was even more elegant than the elevator, with carved and bowlegged European furniture—possibly real antiques, and not just reproductions, if the nightly room rate was any indication: red plush carpet and draperies with contrasting gold accoutrements; a crystal-dripping chandelier; a huge carved wardrobe; a bathroom with all the luxuries of home—if home happened to be a genuine Bel Air mansion; and a very prominent, very large bed.

It was worth it. Milo and she had spent lavish, lovely hours here dining, bathing, and making adorably pleasant, if mediocre, love.

Then there was the balcony. The sliding glass doors opened onto a veranda with gilt railings, seven floors above the bustle of the boulevard. Barbara walked out on it now and looked down—just in time to see Milo's distinctively receding hairline pass beneath on his way to the entry.

Her heart fluttered. He was here! He would be up in the room at any moment. She smiled.

She had just hung her negligee in the closet and made certain that her hair, newly bleached, permed and styled to perfection, was still in place when she heard the door open. She rushed to greet him..

Milo was exactly two inches taller than Barbara's five-five. His black hair was curly, and he kept it cut short, which emphasized how it had begun to ebb at his temples, but no matter. He had the sweetest smile.

Maybe someday, though, she would convince him to get those invisible braces to close the gap between his front teeth.

"Milo, darling," she said, throwing herself into his arms. He held her awkwardly, for she hadn't given him time to set his overnight bag on the floor. She felt it hit her buttocks and gasped.

"Sorry, darling." He drew back, his fuzzy brown brows raised beneath his gold-rimmed glasses. "I mean excuse me, Barbara. After all, love means you never have to say you're sorry."

She forbore from sighing. It would do no good.

Sweet Milo loved his awful adages and puke-inspiring platitudes. She put up with them because she loved him.

She allowed him to place his bag on the floor, then kissed him soundly once more. He tasted of stale coffee. She knew he guzzled cup after cup each day at the office. It was one of his endearing vices.

"Shall we order room service?" she asked.

"Absolutely."

They went over the familiar menu, then ordered a sumptuous feast of French foods whose names Barbara didn't even attempt to pronounce. She let Milo do the talking. He was fluent in five languages, although why he needed to speak Swahili or Tagalog she would never know.

She smiled when he ordered Dom Perignon. She sat back on the gold brocade sofa when he was done. "Did you have a hard time breaking away this evening?"

He shook his head. "Not really. It was important that you and I get together tonight, so I just told my troops that I had to leave on time."

His troops. She loved it when he spoke as if the geeks who worked for him were an army to march off and make money for him.

He sat beside her, and she snuggled up to him. He smelled so appropriately of printer toner. The scent had bothered her at first, but she loved it now. It was so *him*. He still wore his tie knotted tightly at the neck of his white shirt, though he had taken off his sport jacket.

When they were married, she would help him pick a new tailor who didn't have a passion for plaid.

She reached around to loosen his tie. He sighed in contentment.

"So tell me," she whispered, nuzzling his chin with the top of her head. "Why was it so important that we get together tonight?"

He cleared his throat, causing her skull to vibrate. "Well, there comes a time in every relationship when it either has to move forward or—"

A knock sounded at the door.

"That was quick," Barbara said, irritated. What a time for an interruption.

"I told them to bring the champagne first." Poor Milo's tone was apologetic, but she knew he wouldn't say he was sorry.

A liveried waiter wheeled in a huge silver bucket and poured them each a crystal flute filled with effervescent champagne. When he had bowed over his tip and left, they sat again on the sofa.

"Barbara," Milo began, "I asked you here tonight because I had something important to say." His large lower lip jutted, as if he were about to cry.

Poor baby. She knew emotional things were hard for him. She decided to help.

"This has been a very special place for us," she acknowledged. "We came here the first time we made love, then on the first month anniversary of the day we met, and on your thirty-second birthday. All auspicious occasions."

"That's right. So it seemed only fitting that we come here tonight, too." He pulled away from her and stood up.

His wide eyes had narrowed so much that he again appeared as if he were about to break into sobs. Was proposing that difficult for him?

Barbara smiled tremulously. "I understand, sweetheart, and if it's too hard for you to say, then I'll say it." She slid off the sofa and knelt at his feet. "Milo Rice, will you marry me?"

He sucked in his breath. She felt his hands on her shoulders, drawing her up. "Barbara... I... I don't know what to say."

"Just say what's in your heart, dear," she said through gritted teeth, praying he wouldn't resort to the trite, "This is so sudden." She cleared her throat to rid her voice of the irritability she'd just revealed. "I mean," she said more cheerfully, "just say yes."

"No!" This time the jut of his lower lip looked almost belligerent. "That's the point. I didn't come here to ask you to become my lawfully wedded wife, for richer, for poorer—oh, this is just getting worse." His eyes were blinking, and he looked horrified.

And that made Barbara begin to understand. Now *she* was horrified. "Then why did you want to come here?" she asked in a very soft voice.

"To have one last, very pleasant evening with you. You see, I intend to stop seeing you."

"No, Milo. I don't see." Iciness oozed from her lips, but Barbara couldn't help it. Very precisely, she sat back down on the sofa and swigged down her entire glass of Dom Perignon. The bubbles fizzed up her nose, burning it, but she didn't care. She felt the cool liquid flow right where she wanted it: down deep in her belly.

She reached over and poured herself more.

He slowly joined her on the sofa. He lifted her hand, the one not clutching the stem of the champagne flute, and began stroking her knuckles.

She let him. Maybe he'd get turned on, sweep her over to the king-sized bed that now seemed garishly out of place in this monstrosity of an over-decorated room, and make love to her. Realize he couldn't live without her.

Take back his ugly words.

"I won't say I'm sorry, Barbara, since—"

"Yes, yes. Love means you never have to say you're sorry. But are you telling me you don't love me?"

"No, I do. Honest. But I don't see you as the mother of my children. You're too... well, you're so independent. Which is good," he added hastily. "But—"

"But you want a fifties wife, a stay-at-home little woman who'll greet you at the door with her abdomen distended from yet another pregnancy, and tell you about her exciting day cleaning up the baby's belched milk."

"Well...yes." He sounded relieved, as if she had expressed exactly what he wanted to say.

Shit, thought Barbara. "I see." She thought for a moment. "I love you, Milo. And if that's really what you want, I'll try it."

He shook his head sadly. "But that's not you. I know it's not, and you know it's not. So—"

He was interrupted by another knock on the door. Another overdressed waiter entered, wheeled in the cart with a flourish, and offered happily to serve them. He seemed even happier to leave with a hefty tip in his hand.

The respite had given Barbara more time to think. "Milo," she said when they were alone, "what if we just live together for awhile. You'll see how well we'll get along, and then, if it works out, we'll get married."

"No!" he said more sharply than he had ever spoken to her before. He stood facing her, his arms crossed over his scrawny chest, his mouth adamant. "Don't you see? Love is knowing when to let go."

"You and your damned—" She caught herself. "Excuse me. Milo, darling, you can't really mean—"

"I do."

Shit, she thought again. She had intended to hear those two little words tumble from his mouth, but not in this context.

"Now, Barbara," he said. "Let's sit down, eat our dinner, have a pleasant conversation so we'll have fond memories of our last night together."

"Right," she muttered.

"And afterward, if you'd like, we could make love, for old time's sake."

She glared at him. How had she thought he was a different kind of man, old-fashioned, gentlemanly, sweet? He was as ruled by his testosterone as any of them. The oversexed little creep.

Well, she could do as he said, enjoy one last, expensive meal with him. And that would give her more time to think, to plan, to figure out what to do next.

"Okay," she said agreeably. Maybe a smattering of seduction would help. She stood, walked over to him, and gave him a big, deep, soulful kiss. "Fine, Milo," she whispered, and kissed him again.

The earth moved under her feet.

That wasn't simply a statement, she realized. It really was moving.

"Earthquake," Milo squeaked, clutching her arms. She nodded, looking around. There were no good doorways to stand under, no tables or any other suitable shelter to huddle beneath. The chandelier swayed, the cart holding their supper slid across the floor.

The rumbling was loud and seemingly endless—until it ended in a crash. The shaking ceased, too.

"What was that crash?" Milo asked, his voice quaking even after the room had stopped.

"Outside, I think," Barbara said. The window to the

balcony was intact. In fact, though furniture was skewed on the floor, and some hangers and clothes had spilled from open doors of the wardrobe, it didn't appear as if the room had suffered any major damage.

She slid open the glass door and tested the balcony with one foot. It seemed sturdy.

Milo followed her out. They looked around.

People had poured from neighboring buildings onto Sunset. The crash Milo and she had heard was the sound of a couple of cars that had found each other during the quake.

"Wow," Milo said—just as the shaking started again.

"Aftershock!" Barbara shouted. She bolted for the door.

She made it inside. Milo, on the other hand, was clutching the balcony's railing just as it detached from the balcony's floor. He swung out over the seven empty floors of space, then back again.

The railing held by a thread.

Instinctively, Barbara stepped back outside and reached for him. She stood on the tile floor of the blessedly solid balcony. "Milo!" she screamed.

"Barbara," he whispered, clutching her hand as if it were a lifeline. Which it was, for just then the railing parted company with the Sunset Majestic's structure. Barbara screamed. Milo shrieked.

Barbara fell to her knees. She watched the railing tumble and fall and smash with a clang onto the sidewalk seven stories below, narrowly missing a throng of milling pedestrians.

She held onto Milo, straining under the sudden unbearable tug of all his weight. She threw herself flat on her stomach and grabbed Milo's wrist with her free hand.

Jeez. He was heavier than he looked. But she managed, somehow, to hold on. Adrenaline, maybe. Or perhaps all those agonizing hours at the gym were actually paying off.

Milo whimpered. "Please, Barbara, pull me back in."

She tugged a little. Maybe she could manage it.

Her emotions roiled. Fear made her tremble. Her arms felt as if they were about to fall off, right along with Milo. And her thoughts swirled.

"Marry me, Milo," she demanded, nearly out of breath, straining to still hold on.

"Please, Barbara, help me get in."   He was dangling, dangling...

"Promise me now that you'll marry me."

A look of obstinacy crossed his myopic and frightened eyes as they looked up at her. "We'll talk about it—"

"Promise me."

"No," he shouted. "I won't. Barbara, pull me in and we'll— "

"Do you love me at least?" she asked softly. Damn, but her arms hurt.

"Yes," Milo cried. "I love you."

"I love you, too, Milo. Remember what you said?"

"What?"   He looked wild now.   And terrified. "That I won't marry you? Look, Barbara, I—"

"Not that. The other thing."

He just stared at her.

"'Love is knowing when to let go,'" she quoted.

And so she did.

You are now entering Beverly Hills. Don't worry if you missed the famous shield-shaped sign that announces the city limit on Sunset. You don't need it. The fact that you've crossed the line into Millionaire Acres could not be plainer. The median-divided street is suddenly wider and miraculously less congested; the grass is greener; the sentry-like palm trees taller; and people walking—as opposed to driving or being driven—scarcer. It's like opening the farmhouse door and looking out at Oz. Everywhere is the right address in Beverly Hills, and having enough money, fame and power can excuse just about anything. Even murder...

L.A. LATE @ NIGHT

By Paul D. Marks

*Any time you want to you can buy a
little trouble, I can guarantee you that.*

– Steve March Torme & Steve Rawlins

FADE IN:

EXT. DOWNTOWN COURTHOUSE STEPS – LOS
ANGELES – DAY

Cassie Rodriguez smiled her best victory smile.
Moving with the grace and lilt of a dancer, she stepped
toward the gaggle of microphones, where black tape
formed an X. Her mark. ABC. NBC. Fox News. CNN.
Local radio and TV stations from around the country.
Around the world. In her Prada suit-dress and five hundred
dollar haircut she exuded movie star quality. She could
have been on the runway before going into the Academy
Awards as she brushed her long dark hair back from her
face.
Lights flashed on. Cameras whirred. If she'd had
any doubts about her client's innocence, they were blinded
by the lights. The law was as good as Show Biz. The truth
is, she loved it.
Teri Mailer, the Barbie doll reporter for the six

o'clock news, was first up, ready to do her stand-up. Lights snapped on and with them her smile. They weren't the Klieg lights of the movie set Teri had set her heart on when she moved to L.A., but she lit up nonetheless. She knew what she did was just an extension of Show Biz. Wasn't everything?

Teri began: "By now, everyone who hasn't been on the space station knows that film producer Ronald Aberdeen has been accused of murdering and mutilating Hannah Tobin, a Sunset Boulevard prostitute whose body was found behind the infamous Chateau Marmont, just north of Sunset. The stunning conclusion of this dramatic trial came today with Mr. Aberdeen's acquittal." Before she could finish her spiel, a crush of reporters engulfed her and Cassie.

"Cassie, did you think it would go so well for you?" shouted a reporter above the din.

She stared down the cameras. "Of course. It's clear to anyone with eyes that Mr. Aberdeen is innocent."

Deputy D.A.'s Josh Whitman and Dina Larchmont were watching from the sidelines—where they belonged, Cassie thought, after the beating she gave them. She knew what they were thinking, knew they were wishing they could be in the spotlight. She'd been there. Cassie could imagine their dialogue as she postured for the media. *Look at her preen for the cameras*, she imagined Josh saying. *She thinks she's a goddamn movie star. They treat her like one*, Dina would reply, envy and sarcasm dripping from her lips.

Let them talk, Cassie thought. She knew she was the star, especially today. Besides, it was good for her rep if they thought of her that way. Intimidation was half of what it took to be a killer defense lawyer.

The questions came machine-gun staccato, one after another. Cassie knew how to play the game. She'd done it before. Maybe not in as big a case, but the script was pretty formulaic no matter what size the case was.

"What about the mysterious fibers that were found on Hannah Tobin's neck, that could not be matched?" a reporter shouted.

Another reporter barked over the first reporter's question: "What about the body being arranged like Manet's 'Olympia'? And the fact that Mr. Aberdeen used the same conceit in one of his movies?"

"A movie that was seen by millions of people, any one of whom could have copied the idea," Cassie said.

"Did the police plant evidence?   Frame your client?"

More questions shot out. Cassie returned fire.

"Ms. Rodriguez, don't you feel sorry for Hannah Tobin? After all, she was strangled, and brutally mutilated. And what about her family?"

"I have great sympathy for her family. But it's obvious that Mr. Aberdeen is innocent. That's why the jury came back with a not guilty verdict in less than four hours. This is a victory for justice."

"Bitch!" someone in the crowd yelled. "You get off getting killers off." Cassie looked toward the heckler. The woman glared at Cassie. Something struck Cassie inside. Her exterior was cool, calm. Confident. But like a movie set's façade, behind the glittering exterior something was missing. She jammed the thought down as best she could, covered it with another, brighter victory smile.

Teri Mailer did her close. "There you have it, Cassie Rodriguez is on her way to supplanting Johnnie Cochran as the premier criminal defense attorney in Los

Angeles, maybe the country. Nothing can stop her now."

Cassie posed at the top of the courthouse steps, her star shining brightly. Flashes clicked, cameras whirred, reporters proclaimed the news to people across the country.

Flushed with victory and damning her detractors, Cassie escaped to her Jag and headed out to Sunset Boulevard. Every time she hit Sunset the same thoughts flooded her mind. As a little girl she had watched Billy Wilder's movie *Sunset Boulevard* on the Late, Late Show. Living near Chávez Ravine, just a couple blocks from Sunset, she'd thought she would be seeing a movie about her neighborhood. Her friends. Instead she had seen a story about a down on his luck screenwriter who moves from his shabby apartment to a fabulous mansion farther down Sunset. Little girl Cassie hadn't noticed the Grand Guignol character of the mansion's owner. She'd only noticed the mansion. Not long after that, her parents had taken her to the beach. They had driven Sunset all the way from Chávez Ravine to the ocean. She had seen houses like the one in the movie. Houses she vowed she'd live in some day.

What she hadn't realized at the time was that there was a price to pay to be able to live in such a house. Sometimes that price was hanging from a tag that everyone can see. Sometimes it was hidden inside. And like William Holden's character in Wilder's movie, Cassie Rodriguez was *dead* inside. She just didn't know it. In fact, she'd been dying for years, but she didn't know that either. And you would hardly have known it judging by the crowds gathered round her outside the downtown L.A. courthouse on every TV station across the country.

INT.   CASSIE'S JAG – MOVING SHOTS – SUNSET BLVD. – DAY

Cassie's closing argument echoed in her mind as she headed home, west on Sunset, the Hollywood sign glaring down at her. She had to admit it. She loved the attention. The star treatment and power. And she *was* a star. She had proved there was a Santa Claus, at least for Ronald Aberdeen. The killer was still out there, but she had done her job, and Aberdeen was a free man.

He had hugged her when the verdict came in. He let his hands linger on her a little too long. No one could believe how quickly it had come. She was good. Damn good.

But she was tired. The case had been long and wearisome. At the same time she was also wired. She didn't want to go home. She drove on automatic pilot. Her partners and some of the experts they had called were going for a more concrete victory lap at Cachet downtown. She hadn't wanted to go there. Not this time. She liked the attention she knew she'd get there, but even that was wearing thin. And she knew how people talked about her behind her back, even those on her side. They were jealous. Of her cars, her clothes. Her house in Beverly Hills. And she won cases. That was her biggest sin.

She got off bad guys, some of them said. She preferred to think she was seeing that justice was served. Everyone wants to be the hero of their own life movie. She wanted to be the hero of hers. Being a defense lawyer was her way to do that. What was wrong with that?

Bitch! You get off getting killers off!

What *was* wrong with that?   She'd been called names before. They slid off her back. Why was 'this one gnawing at her?

White knuckling the steering wheel, she wondered if the damn light was ever going to change. Had she gotten a killer off? She never asked her clients the question outright. Neither did any other defense lawyer she knew. She'd had doubts about Aberdeen during the trial. What defense attorney didn't have doubts about some clients? Not everyone was innocent. But everyone was entitled to a fair trial. That's what she was there for. And if the police and D.A.'s didn't do their job, well . . .

Nonetheless, was it a pyrrhic victory? It was all just a game, wasn't it? A script all the players were acting out. Justice was a sometime byproduct. Aberdeen was innocent, or at least not guilty. A jury had declared him so. She believed it. She had to.

She saw the neon dancing as she sat waiting for the signal to change. The Café Noir was a dive her assistant Jennifer had told her about. It was just east of the Strip in LAPD country rather than Sheriff's territory. No matter. Most everyone in both departments hated her. But it was a quiet place, a piano bar where there mostly wasn't a piano player, a stage where there were occasional swing bands—occasional as in almost never—and where Jennifer said Scotty from Big Bad Voodoo Daddy came incognito on occasion to have a drink and listen to the music. It was a place where she wouldn't be recognized, and if she was, nobody would care. No Hollywood hot spot here.

INT. CAFÉ NOIR – NO WINDOWS

It was dark and she could have a drink and listen to the kind of old and new swing, jazz and torch music she liked. "I'm a Fool to Want You" was on the juke as she entered, waiting for her eyes to adjust to the dim light.

The inside of the bar was filled with lobby cards and poster repros from film noir movies, *Double Indemnity, The Postman Always Rings Twice, The Dark Corner, Out of the Past.* And from out of the past, the walls, where they showed through, were covered with palm trees and pink flamingos. Other than that, it was dark, as promised. She ordered a Stoli-rocks from the long-haired bartender, who looked out of place in the 1940s setting. He laughed. "Too rich for our blood," he said. And she realized the drinks were also out of the past, Gibsons and Rob Roys, Harvey Wallbangers, and vodka gimlets. She settled for a retro Wallbanger, with a *de rigueur* retro turquoise umbrella and took a seat at a booth in the back. She remembered umbrellas like that in her mom's drinks when she was a child.

She looked at the others in the bar, fortifying themselves on their way home from work to deal with the rigors of family, bills, taxes. Bored kids and raging workers shooting each other on the TV news. She knew there were a lot of bad guys out there. And she defended some of them. Most of those she defended she thought were innocent. But everyone deserved decent representation. Sipping her drink, she thought about all her pro bono work. Aberdeen hadn't been pro bono. As a mini mogul he could afford to pay—and pay he did. Some clients had to support the Jag and Mercedes and the house in Beverly Hills. After all, she'd become accustomed to a certain lifestyle. But money wasn't why she had taken on the case, she'd made good money all along. Nor was it Aberdeen; she'd never liked him. Cassie had known this case would make her a household name. Give her marquee value. She'd wanted that. She had something to prove. To herself. To her parents. To the kids in the neighborhood she'd grown up in. This case proved it.

REVERSE ANGLE – CASSIE'S POV TO SEE A MAN STANDING OVER HER

Cassie looked up to see a man looming over her table. He wasn't a waiter, not with his rumpled suit and glassy eyes. Looked like a B actor in a B picture. Wasn't bad looking, either, if he'd run a comb through his hair. Did he recognize her? Sometimes they wanted autographs. Sometimes they wanted to tell her to go to hell. What did this one want?

"There's no place to sit," he said. "Mind if I join you?"

She looked around. The small bar and handful of tables and booths had filled up. Lots of people delaying going home.

"I'm not in the mood to talk," she said, twirling the umbrella.

"I don't need to talk. Just to sit."

Definitely B movie dialogue. She motioned with her hand. He set his no-brand bourbon on the table—no umbrella here—and sat across the booth from her. His eyes stared off into space.

"I picked your table 'cause you're the prettiest one here," he said without looking at her. "Does that count as sexual harassment?"

He recognized her. He was toying with her. She thought about leaving before the B movie dialogue got worse.

"I didn't mean anything by it. But look around. If you were me, who would you rather sit with?"

Maybe he didn't recognize her.

A Mexican busboy came by to offer them peanuts and pretzels.

"Goddamn illegals," the man said. "Pretty soon we'll be *Mejico-norte.*" He finally looked up at her face. Into her green eyes, which had turned hard and cold. What had he done?

"I'll remember when we take over again, *cabrón.* You know, *senõr, la reconquista*," she said. She could have gotten up and left. She didn't. She wanted to see what he was up to.

He studied her face. His eyes focused and cleared. "Oh God," he laughed. "You're Cassie Rodriguez." All the booze had gone from his voice.

He blushed, but it might simply have been an alcohol rush to his face. "You have green eyes. Why would someone named Rodriguez have green eyes?"

"I'm half Irish." But what he said had struck a chord. Sometimes she didn't know where she belonged. She wasn't fully part of the White Man's world, nor of the Chicano world. She was like an actress playing a different part in different movies. Mexican-American here. Irish woman there. Defense lawyer somewhere else. Sometimes they all came together. Rarely. She wished they would more often.

"Yeah, I think I heard that. Sorry about the Mexican crack." As he spoke, his coat slipped open. She saw a pistol in a shoulder holster. He pulled the jacket closed. She had seen the tape strip with a serial number on the butt of the gun. Cop. Would the B movie clichés never end?

"What's your name, detective?"

"Larry Darrell." Smiling, he pulled his coat tighter.

"So what are you working on tonight, detective?" she said, on a different kind of autopilot now. She wished she had a script to read from. Ad-libbing would have to do.

"I'm searching for truth, justice and the American way." He flipped open his badge wallet.

"So your sitting at this table was no accident, detective." The edge in her voice was sharp. Cassie and the cops, well, that wasn't the proverbial heaven-made match. Damn, she thought. I came here to get away from everything, and now I have to deal with this. She thought about leaving, but where could she go for some peace and quiet after today's news?

"Hell, no. If I knew it was you, I... How 'bout if I buy you a drink and we start over?"

"That would be a first. A cop buying Cassie Rodriguez a drink."

But she let him. And she listened to him tell her about the righteous shooting he'd done a few weeks ago. But since the *victims* were two fifteen year olds, he'd been pulled off active homicide cases and given the cold case detail. A dead end. Some people might be shocked at killing two fifteen year olds. Cassie wasn't. She'd met some fifteen-year-olds who were as hardened as any career criminal.

And he listened to her talk about good judges and bad D.A.s. And she was surprised that she was enjoying the company of this cop, her natural enemy. And pretty much they had a good time. But he didn't congratulate her on her victory today. He thought a murderer had gone free.

"You're not alone," she said.

"Don't you feel bad about setting a murderer like Aberdeen free?"

She bristled. "I didn't set him free, the jury did.

Don't you feel bad about killing two fifteen-year-olds? Did you ask them if they were innocent before shooting?" She went home alone. And so did he.

EXT. CASSIE'S HOUSE – SUNSET BLVD.—NIGHT

   She went home to a Spanish Revival house on Sunset Boulevard in Beverly Hills. Arched columns and tiled porticos. Birds of Paradise and bougainvillea. And, of course, palm trees. But no flamingos. It was almost ten thousand square feet, with real plaster walls and high-beamed ceilings. About ten miles and a thousand light years from the 900 square foot house she had grown up in near Chávez Ravine at the other end of Sunset. She'd left the old 'hood behind. And was proud to be the first person in her family to graduate college, then go on to law school. Now that she could, she wanted to buy her parents a house on the westside, but they wouldn't move. So once a month she went home for homemade tamales and a visit.

                                        CUT TO:

EXT. 1960s STUCCO APARTMENT BUILDING – CARPORTS IN FRONT – NIGHT

   Larry went home to a two-bedroom fake stucco apartment in Palms. Used to be a nice neighborhood bordering Culver City as it did. But it was changing. The whole damn city was changing. Some of it for the better. Some, well... He wasn't one of those cops who was going to eat his gun. He might live (or die) out another cop cliché and drink himself to death. But he wouldn't give the scum he busted the satisfaction of blowing his head off in the middle of the night.

He couldn't sleep. Counting sheep didn't help. Drinking used to, when he drank less. Now it had the opposite effect. No, he'd lie in bed and dream of shooting bad guys in a shooting gallery. Most of the time he hit them dead on.

He'd grown up in L.A., not that far from where Cassie had grown up. Just north of Sunset Boulevard in a fading Hollywood neighborhood. Larry didn't like the way L.A. was changing. Not when you needed a gun for protection just to go to the grocery to buy a can of beer.

* * *

The TV droned in the background as Cassie threw her thousand dollar jacket on the floor of her bedroom. Tossed off her six hundred dollar shoes and let her toes dig into the deep pile carpet. She pulled the Firestar 9mm from her purse and set it on the nightstand. Even with all her power and connections, like almost every other schmuck in L.A., she couldn't get a permit. She carried it illegally. Better to be judged by twelve than carried by six.

She was on every channel. Looking good. She flipped channels. There she was again. This time in a closer shot. Hollywood Cassie, they called her. Like a movie star. But she could see it now. There was triumph in her face, but sadness in her eyes. Maybe no one else would notice. Glad it was a medium shot, not a close-up. She looked at herself in the mirror. Looked away.

She flipped off the TV, put on a Rosemary Clooney CD. Music filled the room, filtering into the bathroom like the scent of jasmine wafting on an L.A. night. She stared at the face above the imported silk blouse. The green eyes shone. She didn't have any lines yet. And her ink black hair was lustrous. Figure still good. But she wondered about herself. On the outside everything looked grand. But like that movie set she'd thought about earlier, the inside was hollow. She was lonely. To Dina Larchmont she probably looked like she had it all. Just like Richard Cory. On the outside he, too, had it all. Everyone was envious of him. Inside, something was missing. Missing enough so that one night he went home and put a bullet in his head. Cassie wasn't ready for that, not by a long shot. But maybe Richard Cory had also gone home to an empty house one evening too many.

"Be My Life's Companion" came on just as she was drifting off, still mostly dressed. Rosemary sang about how people who are lonely can be old at thirty-three.

INT. CASSIE'S OFFICE – DAY

Ronald Aberdeen came to Cassie's office the next day to sign off on a few things. He was a happy man. He made teen slasher movies, even after Columbine. They made tons of money—there was always a market for that stuff. People were jealous. Blamed him and his movies for the ills of the country. He claimed that was why everyone, including the cops, had accused him of the murder. Even tried to frame him. He offered her a large cash tip. She refused it. It meant nothing coming from a man like Aberdeen.

"Hey, you oughta let me screen test you," he told her. "You've got charisma." The look she gave him said, *not me.* "No, not my kind of pix. Real movies. Big budget stuff. I'm thinking of moving over."

"Everyone thinks I'm acting already," she said.

"Are you?"

She didn't answer. She wanted to ask him the same question. Didn't.

She had to get her other briefcase from her car, walked him out to the parking lot.

"Since you won't take money, at least take this token of my appreciation." He gave her a lovely Yamura silk scarf, gently wrapping it around her neck. What could she do but accept it graciously?

She tossed it in her car as he drove off in his Mercedes SUV. She read the bumper sticker on the back: *Hey, hey, NRA, How many kids have you killed today?*

INT. THE CAFÉ NOIR – NIGHT

She'd left work early. Watched TV, looked at some briefs, absentmindedly scarfed down a whole pint of Haagen-Dazs vanilla. It was late, but she hadn't wanted to stay home. She'd showered and put on a pair of jeans and low heels. Headed to the Café Noir. It was almost midnight. She didn't expect it to be crowded. It wasn't. She didn't expect Larry Darrell to be there. He wasn't. But the music was good. The drinks okay.

What was she doing here? She'd left this kind of place long ago. And was she hoping to see Larry? The first thing he'd said to her had insulted her. Maybe he'd just been spouting off. But there was something real about him. Even his redneck honesty was a refreshing change from what she had to deal with every day.

He was the kind of guy who broke the rules. She was the kind of person who almost never did. Maybe that was enough for her to want to see him again.

About twelve-thirty a shadow crawled across her

table. She looked up.

"There's no place to sit," he said. "I was wondering if I could share your table?"

She looked around. The place was almost empty. "Well, if there's no place to sit, detective."

"Slumming?" he said, sitting down.

"I like the music here."

"There's other places that play this stuff."

"Do you have a proprietary interest?"

"Legal mumbo jumbo. Nope. But I've been coming here for years. You might bring in a bad clientele."

"Mexicans or lawyers?"

"Lawyers, of course.   Defense lawyers in particular."

"Are you sure you want to be seen with me, detective? It'll ruin your rep with your fellow cops."

"This ain't a cop bar. Tell you the truth, I'm kinda sick of cop bars. And cops."

Silence loomed between them, broken only by the sounds of Steve March Torme singing "L.A. Late @ Night" on the sound system.

"I say something wrong?"

"No," she said. "It's just that I'm sort of feeling the same way."

"Well, a few days of slumming and you'll want to get back to your ritzy clubs and movie star friends. The anointed."

"Maybe," she said.   "And maybe we have something in common." She waited; he didn't respond. "Maybe we're both tired and looking for something new."

"This ain't nothing new for me."

"Sitting with a defense lawyer is." She sipped her drink. "Maybe we're both a little lonely." The word stumbled from her lips.

"Hollywood Cassie has it all. Lights. Camera. Action. Money. Looks. Fame. What else is there in 21st century America?"

They ordered another round of drinks. Talked about swing music. Torch songs.

"Well, we do have this old music in common," he said.

"We have more than that in common."

"Do we?   Do you really think Aberdeen was innocent? And that the cops framed him?"

That was a conversation stopper.

INT. CASSIE'S BEDROOM – NIGHT

She didn't go back to the Café Noir for a while. Hung with her usual gang of four, attorneys from the office, a couple of experts they used on a regular basis. What was the point? She didn't have anything in common with Larry Darrell or the others at the Noir. Besides, he probably hated her. Sure it was fun for him to have a drink and tease her, but underneath...

She flipped on the TV. A little late night, mindless, guilty pleasure. She surfed channels until the onscreen guide read *Here Today, Dead Tomorrow*. She recognized the title as one of Aberdeen's movies. She'd purposefully avoided them. Before she took him as a client they'd simply held no interest for her. Afterwards, she hadn't wanted them to taint her view of him. He said he'd been framed. Someone had imitated the murder in his movie, laying out the body like a famous painting. The prosecution had wanted to show clips. She had them suppressed. She told herself he'd been framed. She'd believed his alibi and his claim of innocence. Besides, who would be stupid enough to commit a murder like the one in his own movie?

She started to drift off, Aberdeen's movie droning in the background. And then she saw it in her half-sleep/half-dream. The scarf. She lurched up in bed. Heart racing. Palms sweaty. She pushed the hair off her face. She rushed out to her car, grabbed the scarf he'd given her, slid it through her fingers. It was soft, smooth. And maybe just what had been used to kill Hannah.

And maybe it wasn't stupidity, but arrogance. More than a few Hollywood people were known for that.

EXT. RODEO DRIVE – BEVERLY HILLS – DAY

Cassie took the scarf to Gucci on Rodeo Drive. The manager identified it as an extremely rare and expensive Yamura that only a few stores in the whole country carried. Torlino being one. She went there. Aberdeen had bought several of the scarves. She took her Christian Lacroix silk blouse, the silk scarf Aberdeen had given her, and the fiber report on Hannah Tobin to a lab and paid for her own analysis. The fibers of her blouse, expensive silk that it was, were very different from the unknown fibers found on Hannah. But the unknown fibers perfectly matched the Yamura scarf. A rare match made of a rare silk fiber. Her detractors had been right. Aberdeen was guilty. And of how many more?

INT. CAFÉ NOIR – NIGHT

It was a little over a week before she showed again. Late again. Almost midnight. She took an empty table.

Larry sent the bartender over to her table with a Harvey Wallbanger. She waved thanks, but didn't come over. He thought that would be it. He put a quarter in the jukebox. "Green Eyes" by Jimmy Dorsey came on. A few minutes later she was standing next to his table.

"This place is getting too crowded. Do you mind sharing your table?" she said. He grinned and she sat down.

"Slumming again? I didn't think I'd see you in here," he said.

"If I'm slumming, then you must be coming up in the world. Besides, I didn't think you'd want to see me after our last conversation."

"Hey, lady, you do what you gotta do. I do what I do."

"And never the twain shall meet."

"They shall meet in the dead of night in the Café Noir. The night people."

She lifted her glass. "To the night people." He clinked his glass on hers, jiggling the little umbrella.

"To L.A. late at night."

They drank.

"Can I ask you something?" she said.

"Shoot—well, not literally. I know how you feel about cops."

She smiled at his joke. The smile was real—he saw it in those delicious green eyes—but she turned deadly serious again. "I'll trust you with something if you answer my question. Deal?"

"Deal."

"I carry a gun illegally. A Firestar nine millimeter." She opened the purse she'd bought at a gun show, spread apart the secret velcroed compartment, and there it was.

She loved it.

He didn't look up from his drink. "You and everyone else in L.A."

"You could bust me. And wouldn't that be a feather in your cap? Busting the hated Cassie Rodriguez, bane of bad cops everywhere."

"Bane of good cops, too." Larry put his hand out, palm up, waiting for the pistol. At first she wasn't sure what to do. Finally, she put it in his hand. He hefted it. He dropped the magazine, filled with 9mm hollow points. He went to clear the chamber, but there was nothing to clear. The bar was nearly empty and those who were there couldn't have cared less about those metal-on-metal sounds they heard. He moved the slide back and forth, with difficulty. "It's so dry the slide barely moves. Needs oil."

Cassie's tensed muscles relaxed.

"Dead gun," he said. "Dead defense attorney." He pulled a small plastic bottle from his pocket, squirted oil on the slide and slide rails. Moved it back and forth. Put the gun back together. "Oh, and if you're going to carry it illegally, you might as well go all the way, cocked and locked." He pushed the magazine into the grip, jerked the side, and a shell jacked into the chamber. "Now you're ready."

"You're not going to bust me?"

"Ask your question, then I'll decide."

"Have you ever planted evidence?"

He didn't answer, looked away from her.

"Have you ever framed anyone?" she said.

Finally he said, "Has anyone you got off ever turned out to be guilty?" He downed his drink. "Get to the point."

She pulled the Yamura scarf out of her purse and

pushed it across the table. He looked at it quizzically.

"The unknown fibers," she said. "Aberdeen gave this to me." She knew what she was doing. This could be the end of her career if it came out. Maybe even worse than that. Was this equivalent to Richard Cory putting the gun to his head? She didn't think so. Was it like the William Holden character floating face down in the pool in *Sunset Boulevard?* She hoped not.

He was familiar enough with the case to know what she was talking about. He said, "Why don't you bring it to the D.A.?"

"I know how the system works."

"What do you want?"

"Justice."

"Flamingo" by Duke Ellington and Herb Jeffries came on. "Shall we dance?" he asked.

DISSOLVE TO:

INT. BEDROOM – LARRY'S APT. – NIGHT

The TV was on. Teri Mailer beamed out at Larry and countless thousands. A star in her own right. "Ronald Aberdeen, who five months ago was acquitted of the murder of Hannah Tobin, has been convicted of the killing of Jeri Ynez, whose body was found less than a week after Mr. Aberdeen walked free," she said into the camera.

Sometimes there's a legal decision and sometimes there's justice, Larry thought, as he poured himself a bourbon. He thought it would help him sleep. He knew he needed sleep. He just didn't like to give up control like that. He thought about what he and Cassie had done. That certainly wouldn't keep him from sleeping. It had been easy enough for him to rub the Yamura scarf on Ynez's dead neck.   And easy enough to plant the scarf at Aberdeen's. Who knew? Maybe Aberdeen really did kill her? If not, he had to pay for the one he had. Maybe someone else skated on this one, but he'd get caught up sooner or later too.

Teri Mailer droned on, "Aberdeen shouted his innocence, but the evidence was overwhelming, thanks to the skilled detective work of officer Larry Darrell, who found the rare silk Yamura scarf that matched the unknown fibers on Ms. Ynez's neck. The scarf clinched it for the jury." Now Larry was a star. Maybe this would get him off the cold case detail.

He wondered about him and Cassie. Would they ever see each other again? Would he face her in a courtroom someday? Would she show up at the Café Noir some long, dark night? He didn't know.

INT. CASSIE'S BEDROOM – NIGHT

Cassie threw her nine hundred dollar jacket on the floor and flipped on the TV. Teri Mailer stood in front of a deserted courthouse. Not a soul in sight, but she was doing a *live* stand-up.   That was all that mattered. "Aberdeen is one of the few who can afford that scarf and he had bought several," the reporter said. "One has to wonder if Ronald Aberdeen would still be a free man if he had had Cassie Rodriguez defending him again. I had the opportunity to speak with Ms. Rodriguez earlier today and asked her about the case."

The station cut to an insert: Teri and Cassie. "Why aren't you repping Mr. Aberdeen this time?" Teri asked. On the TV the camera moved in for a close-up. Cassie turned away and went into the bathroom. She knew the real answer, not the BS one about an overwhelming caseload that she'd given to the reporter.

INT. CASSIE'S BATHROOM – CLOSE-UP – ON CASSIE IN MIRROR

She looked better than she had in a long time. Alive. She hadn't shared Richard Cory's fate or William Holden's fate in *Sunset Boulevard.* She'd resurrected herself. She thought about Larry, wondered if he'd be at the Café Noir tonight. She stared into the mirror—could a camera really see into one's soul? She wasn't afraid anymore of anyone seeing inside her. Seeing her up close. She smiled her best victory smile—a real one this time, not a Hollywood façade.

Still smiling into the mirror, she whispered: "Mr. DeMille, I'm ready for my close-up."

FADE OUT.

The street is getting narrower now, a little curvier, and more rustic. Large apartment and condo buildings line the sides of Sunset Boulevard—oh, there are still mansions here, but they are harder to spot. This is Brentwood, and yes, we will be crossing Rockingham Drive, but we will not stop. That house is no longer there anyway, having become one more ghost in a city full of them. Brentwood is one of the last spots of civilization before Sunset Boulevard gives way to the brushy wilds of Rustic and Temescal Canyons. This hilly, upscale residential area remains the zip code of choice for many, despite its history of being plagued by a variety of Southern California natural disasters.

As well as a few that are not so natural...

LEAP OF FAITH

By Anne Riffenburgh

It's been said there's a novelty gene, a quirk in DNA that's linked to risk-taking and a craving for change. This theory has been used to account for a variety of behaviors—everything from skydiving to arranging lounge furniture artistically on the bottom of a hotel pool. For a long time I thought this gene had bypassed me. And then something happened that altered my perception.

Over the past year, I'd experienced enough change to last a few lifetimes—none of it by choice. I'd lost a husband, suffered a miscarriage, and coped with the tragic death of a co-worker from the ER. As an employee assistance counselor I'd spent countless hours helping others bring their addictions, dysfunctional relationships, and anxieties under control. Now I felt as if my own life was spinning hopelessly off its axis.

All of which helps explain how I came to be driving along Bundy Avenue at seven-thirty on a gray morning in February. I'd spent too many Sundays lying around with the shades drawn, feeling sorry for myself. Maybe if I took charge of my own life, the fates might be less inclined to use it as their personal playground. With that thought, I'd pulled on my hiking boots, grabbed my windbreaker, and jumped into my battered BMW convertible. Then I'd headed north out of Santa Monica before I could change my mind.

From Bundy, I made a left turn onto Sunset Boulevard, weaving through upscale Brentwood toward

Temescal Canyon in Pacific Palisades. The top was down
and the biting wind whipped my hair into wild ringlets.
For the first time in weeks I felt alive.

As I pulled into the canyon's nearly empty parking
lot, a dark SUV peeled out, missing me by inches. I caught
a glimpse of sunglasses and a baseball cap.

"Jerk!" I shouted. "Jerk of all jerks!"

I took a deep breath, vowing not to let one idiot ruin
my day. After all, this was a place for calming down, not
stressing out.

According to locals, "Temescal" was an Indian
word for sweat lodge.   Long ago, the Indians had
frequented this area, seeking rejuvenation of the mind,
body, and spirit. It was easy to see why. The eucalyptus
trees were shrouded in mist and fragile puffs of dandelions
dotted the landscape. A fat beetle-bug scuttled out of my
way.

Walking briskly, I started up the trail that led to the
waterfall. I hadn't gone more than five hundred yards when
I heard someone yelling for help. The voice sounded
young, and I hesitated, wondering if it was a joke. Then
the cry was repeated, and there was no mistaking the tone
of desperation. I broke into a jog.

"Where are you?" I hollered.

"Over here! Behind the cabin."

Temescal Canyon boasts a handful of slightly
dilapidated bungalows that can be rented out to scout
troops and business groups. I darted behind one and
stopped cold.

A man and woman had been flung against the
foundation. The man's neck was twisted at an ugly angle.
He was dead. Just yards away, the woman lay on her side,
moaning softly. Dark, tangled hair had fallen across her

face, but an ugly cut was visible on one exposed cheek. A trickle of blood escaped from the side of her mouth.

A teenaged boy crouched next to them. He rushed toward me, nearly tripping over his own feet. Freckles stood out against his pale skin like small constellations, and his breath came in jagged bursts.

I grabbed him by the shoulders to steady him. "What's your name?" I asked in an effort to ground him further.

"Josh," he gasped.

"I'm Charity Brandt. What happened, Josh? Do you know these people?"

"No. I just found them like that."

"Okay, we've got to get help. Can you flag someone down while I stay with them?"

He took off running. While he was gone, I tucked my windbreaker around the woman. "Hang in there," I urged. Her eyelids fluttered. There was no other response.

Within minutes Josh was back with a ranger. "Lord have mercy, will you look at this." She met my gaze grimly. "Paramedics should be here soon." Even as she spoke, we heard the wail of sirens in the distance. "What happened?"

"I don't know. I ran over when I heard Josh yelling for help."

"I'm not sure either," Josh echoed. "I was on my way back from the waterfall when a man yelled, 'Hey!' and a woman screamed. I think they must've fallen from the path."

"Or been pushed," the ranger said softly.

I shivered in the thin sunlight. The drop was steep. They were probably airborne for part of the fall. I picked up the thread of questioning.

"After you hiked down here, Josh, did you see or hear anything else unusual?"

"Not really. Oh, one weird thing. Somebody was burning rubber in the parking lot. The lady kind of woke up. She said, 'car' and grabbed my arm. Maybe she thought the attacker was getting away."

My mind flashed back to the SUV. I wasn't sure of the color, much less the make and model. And I'd barely caught a glimpse of the driver. Some witness I'd make.

"Anything else?"

He tucked his shaggy, wheat-colored hair behind large, protruding ears. "Well, then she mumbled some guy's name. 'John. Where's John?' That was it."

The sirens intensified as emergency personnel poured into the parking lot. Soon paramedics were bending over the victims, while police officers hustled the three of us to one side, and began questioning us separately. I had just gotten to the part about the SUV when one of the paramedics pulled a driver's license from the woman's pocket.

"Her name's Donna Medvin."

I gasped. The stocky cop in front of me glanced up sharply. "Does that mean something to you?"

"Yes. Yes, it does."

Donna Medvin was one of the surgeons at the hospital where I worked.

* * *

If Mondays have a reputation for being grim, this one could serve as a prototype. I was still shaken from the scene I'd witnessed, but I hadn't seen much point in sitting around at home. With the exception of my supervisor, I'd told no one at work of my involvement. Now a variety of faces surrounded me — some tearstained, others stoic. All had been acquainted with Dr. Donna Medvin, one of the top surgeons at Brentwood Memorial Hospital. Most had heard the news Sunday night, when local stations broke the story of the brutal ambush of Dr. Medvin and her husband, Jonathan, a prominent architect. The husband was dead at the scene, while Dr. Medvin succumbed to internal injuries in the ambulance.

We were in the conference room on Station 45, the medical-surgical unit where Dr. Medvin admitted most of her patients. The unit supervisor, Lucy Wolkowski, had paged me at the employee assistance office. Her staff was stunned. Would I run a supportive session? The nurses could drop in as their patient care demands allowed.

"This is unbelievable," one of the aides was saying. "I just saw Dr. Medvin on Friday. She was so happy about having the weekend off."

"I'll bet," commented the unit secretary, a bird-like woman who pursed her lips as if she'd just bit into a lemon. "She'd had an ugly run-in with Dr. Ribicki that morning. Everyone was talking about it."

"What happened?" I asked, exchanging glances with Lucy Wolkowski. In a profession where large egos were prevalent, Dr. Michael "I-got-it-all" Ribicki was the odds-on favorite for the title of most arrogant and abrasive.

It was Lucy who answered. "Let's just say that a certain surgeon had been warned several times by the Chief of Surgery—our own Dr. Medvin—to provide proof that he'd gotten his medical license renewed. By Friday he still hadn't produced it. Dr. Medvin marched into the OR as he was closing up his patient and suspended him."

One of the male nurses whistled softly. "I bet that went

over well. Maybe the cops should look at Dr. Ribicki's
alibi." An IV started beeping, and he rose to check it. "You
never know what will set someone off."

The conversation shifted then, with several staff
members sharing feelings of grief, as well as increased
anxiety over their personal safety. As we finished up, I
told Lucy I wished I could have been of more help.

"Listen, it was great. We needed to hear that these
feelings are normal. Besides, if our nurses can have five
minutes of someone focusing on them, it's a huge bonus."

I made a quick stop at my office to pick up my
lunch. With luck, I could grab twenty minutes on the back
patio before my beeper went off again. As if on cue, the
small plastic box began vibrating. Damn. I checked the
extension. Double damn. It was the Medical Staff
Office—not a summons that should be postponed. I
stopped at a house phone and punched in the number.

"This is Greg Franklin."

I cringed. "Charity Brandt. Did somebody—"

"I paged you. We have a problem. Could you stop
by and see my secretary?"

"I'm on my way."

The atmosphere in the Medical Staff Office always
seemed more rarified than the rest of the hospital. I wished
belatedly that I'd stashed my lunch somewhere—a
noticeable smell of peanut butter was emanating from it.
An older woman in cashmere and pearls glanced up from
her computer screen. "Are you the EAP social worker?"
she inquired primly. I nodded. "They're expecting you.
She tilted her head, and her upswept hairdo swayed back
and forth as if it had been retrofitted. "Second door on the
right."

Dr. Franklin sprang to his feet, pushing a lock of

blond hair off his forehead. The gesture was one I'd seen him perform numerous times—usually in the presence of some young, impressionable female. Someone must've told him once that they found it sexy.

"Thanks for coming over," he said, clasping my hand and giving my chest the once over. "Just doing my job," I said shortly. This guy could benefit from a good smack to the groin.

"This is my secretary, Melinda Kerr."

Melinda was seated upon a sofa opposite Dr. Franklin's massive mahogany desk. She was a big-boned woman of about thirty, attractively dressed in a navy suit that set off her dark hair and eyes.

"Hello. Please don't get up," I said, planting myself in an uncomfortable wingback chair. Dr. Franklin retreated to his desk.

"I know who you are," Melinda said, with a tentative smile. "I've just never needed to see you before."

"What's going on?"

She twisted a tissue. "You've heard about Dr. Medvin, of course."

I nodded.

"Naturally that's hit us pretty hard, but we were all doing our best to get our work done. Then I got the phone call."

"What kind of phone call?"

"A threatening one," Dr. Franklin put in. "We've already notified the police."

I turned back to Melinda. "What happened?"

"I got my pad and pen ready like I always do." As she spoke, she systematically shredded the tissue and patted it into a little pile. If I threw in my lunch we could start a compost heap.

"Then I heard a man's voice," she said, hesitating.

"What did he say?" I prompted.

She squeezed her eyes shut. "He said, 'Your stupid doctors killed my mother. These murders were payback—believe it.'"

After that bombshell, I'd spent twenty-five minutes reassuring Melinda. Yes, it was possible she'd talked to Dr. Medvin's killer. But it was also possible the caller was simply some nutcase excited by the publicity. No, I didn't think she was a target. I encouraged her to look at talking to the police as a positive experience. Perhaps her account might help them in some way. And, by being active and involved, she might ease her own feelings of victimization.

I'd made it out to the patio, and was just biting into an apple, when my beeper began its St. Vitus's dance again. At Brentwood Memorial, there was no place to hide.

Minutes after I responded to the page, a plainclothes detective was making his way toward me. A woman at the next table spotted him first. "Hubba hubba," she said to her seatmate. "Hand me a biscuit and let me sop up *that* gravy."

He *was* good-looking. In the old days I might even have been interested. "Are you Charity Brandt?" he inquired.

"That's me."

"I'm Detective Antony Barcelona," he said, flashing his shield. "LAPD. I have some questions." Ducking under the metal tabletop umbrella, he folded his lanky frame into a seat next to me and pulled out a copy of a police report. For several minutes he quizzed me on my version of Sunday's events at Temescal Canyon. Next he brought up Melinda Kerr's crank call and my meeting with her. Finally, he touched on the most painful topic of all.

"I understand your late husband, Neil Brandt, was an internist on staff here."

"That's right," I responded in surprise.

"What were the circumstances of his death?"

I looked at him sharply. "What does that have to do with your investigation?"

"Please answer the question, Mrs. Brandt. It may be important."

I took a deep breath. "My husband was sixteen years my senior. Still, neither of us ever expected he'd have a massive heart attack at the age of forty-seven. By the time we got to the ER he was in bad shape. They did surgery, and he spent five days post-op on the CCU."

It seemed a tame recitation of one of the most grueling events of my life.

"Who did the surgery?"

"One of our top cardiac guys, Richard Laine."

"What happened?"

"Neil was stable and recuperating nicely. Then suddenly, he was gone." I picked up my half-eaten apple and took aim at a trash can ten feet away, drilling the shot. "They were pretty sure he threw a blood clot to the brain."

"But not entirely sure."

I didn't bother to mask my irritation. "Look, I declined an autopsy. What was the point? My husband was dead. No amount of information could change that. Now I'd like to know what *your* point is, detective."

Detective Barcelona leaned forward and fixed his gaze full on my face. His eyes were whiskey-brown, flecked with gold. "Here's what it looks like from where I sit."

"I'm listening."

"Five months ago, one of your ER doctors was run

down in a crosswalk on a well-lit street on the way to the parking lot. No skid marks. We haven't located the driver. Yet."

"I know all this," I cut in. "And I'd appreciate it if you'd speak of Dr. Cooper as a human being instead of just one more unsolved statistic."

"Fair enough," he said. "And I'd appreciate it if you'd let me finish."

I opened my mouth, took note of his granite jaw, and promptly closed it again.

"Yesterday, Donna Medvin, one of your surgeons, was ambushed with her husband while hiking. Today, a secretary in the Medical Staff Office received a call that suggests physicians may be the target of a disgruntled family member."

"But that couldn't possibly be related to Neil's death." Detective Barcelona shrugged his broad shoulders. "It's unlikely anyone would have sneaked into your husband's room to mess with his recovery. But stranger things have happened."

If those words hit me like a blow, I could hardly believe what came next.

"The thing is, Mrs. Brandt, you're in the thick of it. You were up in those hills yesterday. You were the one who counseled that secretary today. Your late husband was a doctor, and doctors are dying."

"Look," I said hotly. "I know you get paid to develop all kinds of theories. But you're way off base if you think I had anything to do with these killings." I stood up fast, narrowly avoiding hitting my head on the rim of the umbrella. "I think this interview is over."

He was beside me in half a second, standing so close I had to fight the impulse to step backward. "No, it's over when I've confirmed your home telephone number and address. I may have more questions later on."

Knowing that it would only make things worse if I refused, I spat out the information, which he noted on a small pad.

"Thank you for your time," he said evenly, handing me a business card. "I'll be in touch."

I shoved the card in my pocket without looking at it. "By the way, there's something else you should know. I had a miscarriage three weeks after my husband died. When you figure out how I pulled off this diabolical plot, make sure you work that in too."

By the time I got to my office, I was crying. With considerable effort, I pulled myself together and saw my afternoon appointments. By the time I got home I had a raging headache. On Tuesday morning I got out of bed long enough to call in sick. Then I crawled back under the comforter and stayed there. I had no intention of going to work for the rest of the week. It was time to take care of me. Everybody else could go to hell.

By Wednesday I was feeling calmer. Sipping a cup of tea, I walked out onto the balcony off my bedroom and sat in one of the white wrought iron chairs. Below me, turquoise water shimmered in the pool Neil and I had designed three years ago, as a wedding present to ourselves. Edged in Jerusalem stone, the pool curved through the yard with lines as pure and clean as any Henry Moore sculpture. Usually, I felt a sense of serenity as I gazed at it, but not today. Detective Barcelona's words had robbed me of something precious and intangible—peace of mind.

Setting down my cup with a clatter, I reached a decision. It was time to follow my own advice: get proactive. Reject the role of victim.

Twenty minutes later, I was making my way down the hospital's main corridor toward the medical staff office. Since I was technically out sick, I kept my head low and prayed I wouldn't run into my supervisor.

"Just the person I wanted," I said as Melinda Kerr glanced up. "How are you doing?"

"Better, thanks. No more crazy phone calls."

"Glad to hear it." I perched on the edge of her desk. "Say, I have a question for you."

"Shoot."

"I heard that Dr. Ribicki had his medical privileges suspended. What does that mean? I know he can't do surgery. Can he conduct his own rounds?" The question was important because Dr. Ribicki had a reputation for early weekend rounds, followed by 18 holes of golf. If the guy had been checking wounds and dressings at 7:30 Sunday morning, it would pretty much rule him out as a suspect.

"As far as I know he can still do rounds," Melinda replied. "But when he writes an order, another doctor has to co-sign it. Is that what you wanted to know?"

"Yeah, thanks." I started to get up, but she stopped me.

"Say, Charity, this is none of my business, but is it true you were at Temescal Canyon the day Dr. Medvin was killed?"

The question floored me. "Where did you hear that?"

"I hate to tell you, but it's all over the hospital."

I thought back to the heated exchange I'd had with Detective Barcelona. My heart sank as I realized we'd been in earshot of several employees. That was Brentwood

Memorial: just one big high school.

My next stop was Station 45.   Fortunately, the medical-surgical unit was bustling, so nobody paid the slightest bit of attention to me.   I found a lone chart bearing Dr. Ribicki's name and flipped to the progress section, tracing back to Sunday's date.   There, next to Dr. Ribicki's scrawled note, was the information I was most interested in: the time.   The entry read 8:45 a.m., which meant he could have had ample opportunity to ambush Dr. Medvin before hotfooting it over to the hospital.   That made him a suspect in my book.

Despite my success, I couldn't ignore other theories.   I had one more stop to make.   As I entered the crowded waiting room of my late husband's office, neither of the receptionists looked up from their calls, but Patricia DeAnda, the office manager, spotted me immediately.

"Charity!   Hold on a sec."   The door to the back office swung open, and she shepherded me into her cubicle. "Sit down, sit down," she urged in her trademark growl. "Let me see you.   How the heck are you?"

"Hanging in there."

"Still too skinny," she said, giving me the once over.   "Come by and join me and Joe next week for my famous eggplant parmesan.   Complexion's all right though—you've got that English rose thing going, the way Princess Diana did.   Say, do you want me to let the docs know you're here?"

"They're busy.   Don't bother.   Actually, I came to ask a favor."

"Name it."

"I need the database of all Neil's patients before he died."

She looked speculative.   "A cop was in here

yesterday, asking for the exact same thing. Detective with some Spanish name, like Madrid."

"Barcelona?"

"That would be the one. Yummy."

"Look Pat, do you remember when Dr. Cooper was killed in that hit-and-run?" She nodded. "And of course, you heard about Dr. Medvin's murder. Well, the police seem to think those things may have some link to Neil."

She snorted derisively. "That's ridiculous. All those doughnuts they eat must have replaced their brains." She sat down at her computer. "But if you want it, you got it. How far back do you want me to go?"

"How far back did Detective Barcelona go?"

"A year."

"Then that's what I want, too. And Pat, could you jot down the names of any patients or family members who've struck you as difficult?

"You got it, sugar."

That evening I downloaded the disk onto my computer and scanned the information. If a patient had died, an "e" for expired should be on record. After several hours, I stopped in disgust. My God, there must be two thousand names here, not to mention a couple hundred "e" entries. That was the downside to having lots of frail, elderly patients.

I picked up the handwritten notes with the heading, "Odd Ducks/Problem People." Pat was too much. Ten names were people whose accounts had gone to collection. Twelve bore short individual descriptions, such as, "constant complainer," "misses her appointments," and "husband is an S.O.B." By ten o'clock I was ready for bed.

Despite the fact that I was tired, I tossed and turned until well after midnight. Eventually, I fell into a fitful, dream-filled sleep. One minute I was floating peacefully above a carnival of laughing children. The next, I was careening wildly in a red bumper car with Neil sprawled in the back seat. Suddenly, we were struck violently from behind. Spinning around, I caught sight of a shadowy figure at the wheel of a dark blue bumper car. Weaving wildly, I tried to shake him off—to no avail. With a tremendous *SMACK,* he hit us again, sending us straight for the edge of a sheer drop-off, as I tried frantically to unbuckle Neil's seatbelt.

Neil opened his eyes. "Let go, baby. Jump." I hesitated, not wanting to leave him. "Jump!"

I awoke with a start, my heart racing. Something about the dream tugged at the corners of my consciousness, but for the life of me I couldn't put my finger on it.

I spent the day printing out data entries on each of Neil's deceased patients—a grand total of two hundred and twenty-seven. In the late afternoon, I gathered up the info on "the stiffs," as well as the short dossiers on Pat's "odd ducks"—and headed for the hospital. I wanted access to my office computer.

Logging on, I quickly accessed Clinipac, the patient data program used by the hospital. Starting with the names from Pat's list, and moving on to the "e-ticket" entries, I brought up the data sheets containing the standard info—name, address, phone number and contact person—as well as diagnosis, hospital admission dates and attending physicians. I wanted to see if any of Neil's patients had a connection to Dr. Cooper in the ER, as well as to Dr. Medvin.

I didn't bother skimming for matches now. I just brought up data sheets and clicked on the "print" icon. After several hours, I'd made a good dent in the project, but my shoulders ached, and my eyes were on fire. Should I keep going or come back tomorrow? I heard a key in the lock, and a janitor popped his head in the door, startling us both. That settled it—time to hit the road.

Back at home, I fixed a baked potato with all the trimmings—green pepper, bacon, and cheddar cheese—Pat should see me putting away the calories now. After a hot bath, I curled up in bed with a glass of wine and a thick sheaf of computer printouts. Using a yellow marker, I highlighted anyone who had been in the ER or an in-house patient of Dr. Medvin during the appropriate time period. By midnight I'd discovered a few that met the first criterion or the second—but not both. Finally, I turned off the light.

When sleep came, it was deep and replenishing. I woke up as the dark velvet of the night sky began to bleed into the gauzy gray of early morning. The digital clock said five-thirty. That had been a decent night—no carnival, cliff, or bumper car had disturbed my dreams. I snuggled into the pillow.

And then it hit me. *Bumper car.*

Sitting bolt upright, I recalled Josh's voice at the canyon. *She said, 'car' and grabbed my arm.* What if that were accurate, but what if Dr. Medvin hadn't been referring to the squealing tires of an SUV?

What if she'd been uttering the killer's name?

Turning on the light, I rifled through the stack of papers at the side of the bed. I scanned the names looking for any kind of variation on "Car"—Carr, Carson, Carter, Carmichael—anything with those three letters.

When I finally found what I was looking for, I stared in disbelief. There it was—the name Dr. Medvin had tried to convey so desperately: not *Car*, but *Kerr.* The hospital data sheet showed back-to-back ER admits for 67 year old Delores Kerr, surgery with Dr. Medvin, and a serious diagnosis—metastatic cancer. A crosscheck turned up an "e" next to the same name on the printout from Neil's office.

I ran my finger down the page to "contact person" and stopped cold. Three simple words gave me all the confirmation I needed: "Melinda Kerr, daughter."

Melinda Kerr, killer.

My God, just two days ago, I'd perched on Melinda's desk in the Medical Staff Office and let her quiz me about my presence in Temescal Canyon. No wonder she'd seemed curious. She must have been desperate to know if I'd seen anything that could implicate her.

With my heart beating wildly, I leaped out of bed and rummaged through the closet for the jacket I'd worn on Monday. Seconds later, I was holding Antony Barcelona's business card in my hand. Punching in numbers on the phone, I prepared to leave a message on his voice mail.

A deep male voice picked up on the first ring. "Detective Barcelona."

"What are you doing there?" I said, without thinking.

"I guess I couldn't sleep either." He sounded amused. "Who is this?"

"Charity Brandt. Listen, I need to talk to you. I've figured out—"

Down the hall a floorboard creaked, followed by the unmistakable sound of footsteps.

"Someone is inside my house!" I said hoarsely.

Melinda Kerr stood in my bedroom doorway, blinking, as her eyes grew accustomed to the light. She wore tight black leather gloves that ran nearly to the elbow, and in her right hand she held a knife.

Oh God, I thought, I'm about to be killed by a woman in opera gloves. I bit back hysterical laughter.

"Hello, Charity," she said pleasantly. "I needed to see you again."

In response, I threw the phone straight at her head, but she batted it to the floor with the grace of a natural athlete. I turned and scrambled through the French door onto the balcony, closing the door behind me, wedging one of the wrought iron chairs under the door handle.

Melinda reached the French door in three strides and kicked her boot through a pane of glass. I felt a sharp sting below my ear. The chair scraped forward several inches. I leaped at it, planting my back against the cold balcony wall and wedging my feet against the chair. Gone was the tentative secretary. The woman before me was focused and determined.

"Is that any way to treat your houseguest?" she asked mockingly, speaking through what was left of the French door.

"How did you get in here?"

"Through a downstairs window. I've been here for an hour, watching you sleep, waiting for you to awaken." Her words slammed into me. I struggled to breathe, but it was as if the air around me had turned thick and poisonous.

"There was no threatening call," I gasped. "You made it up, didn't you?"

A Mona Lisa smile played at her lips.

"Tell me one thing, " I said desperately. Did you have anything to do with my husband's death?"

That surprised her. "You mean did I tamper with his IV or smother him with a pillow? I'm afraid not. That was the hand of God. That was the beginning."

"What do you mean?" I glanced around frantically

for some kind of weapon. There was nothing.

"Your fool of a husband was my mother's internist. He completely missed her cancer diagnosis. Then came that stupid ER doctor—he turned her away—sent her home with antacid. When he finally readmitted her, she was doubled over in pain. The brilliant Dr. Medvin had a crack at her next—and ended up killing her on the operating table." She laughed bitterly. "Do no harm. That's the first rule of medicine, isn't it? But they harmed her every step of the way." Her dark hair fell forward, shielding her face like a raven's wing. "There was no way to undo their mistakes. All that was left was justice. When your husband died, it was an omen."

Melinda Kerr tossed back her hair and watched me intently. Her eyes were deep pools of anger and pain. "You know what that omen meant, don't you, Charity?"

I did know. And I knew she wanted me to say it. "That they should all die," I answered quietly.

She nodded with satisfaction. "Exactly."

I heard the wail of sirens and knew Detective Barcelona was on his way. I felt a pang of foolishness at my earlier reluctance to give him my address. Then fear rose like bile as I realized all of that hardly mattered now. By the time the police got here it would be too late.

"Now," Melinda went on, "you and I have some unfinished business."

"But I had nothing to do with your mother's death!"

Her face took on an expression of impatience. "I know that, Charity. That's not the reason you have to die. You were just unlucky enough to get involved." She stroked the tip of the knife, and I watched mesmerized as the blade shone against the darkness of her leather glove.

"Besides, your husband's death cheated me. It's

only fair that you should stand in for him."

In a flash, I was on my feet. I was trembling with fear and cold, but I was beyond feeling it. There was a crash and the chair went flying. I was on the wall now, looking down, my bare feet digging into the stucco. There was concrete below, then Jerusalem stone, then pool.

There was no way I could make it. There was no other way out.

I swear I heard his voice. "You can do it, Charity. Jump."

I leaped then, with all the strength I could muster, closing my eyes, bracing myself for the inevitable impact of concrete, but there was only water—sweet, freezing, life-affirming water. I hit the bottom hard, pushed off, broke the surface, and swam dazedly to the side. There was a man waiting for me. He extended his hand and hauled me, dripping, out of the pool.

Detective Barcelona wrapped his jacket around my quaking shoulders. "Charity suffereth long and is kind," he quoted softly.

"Milton?"

"First Corinthians," he corrected, pressing a handkerchief firmly against the cut on my neck. "Twelve years of Catholic school."

I glanced up at the balcony. Three uniformed officers were grappling in the shadows with a dark and malevolent figure, the figure of my dreams. I looked away, over Antony Barcelona's shoulder, to the east. The sun was up on the horizon, weaving muted pinks and lavenders into the early morning clouds—bringing soft light, fresh hope, and the shimmering promise of a new day.

Look out the window...it's almost hard to believe we are still in Los Angeles. This part of Sunset winds around like a switchback, cutting through one of the most rustic, underdeveloped and, at night, darkest parts of the city. Still, let's pull over for a moment. That drive through the trees on the left is the entrance to Will Rogers State Historic Park, which is laid out around the legendary humorist's last Hollywood home. The artifact-filled house, the grounds, the hiking trails and the polo field have been maintained exactly as Will left them in 1935, the year of his death. It is a shrine to one of the nation's best-loved figures.

Of course, not everyone in show business has had as pure and noble a history...

BLACK AND RED AND DEAD ALL OVER

By Gabriella Diamond

Believing the adage that there was no life east of Beverly Hills, Bull Fortson steered his black Rolls up Sunset's western beginning, through the upper middle-class neighborhood of Pacific Palisades, with its manicured yards, stately two hundred year old eucalyptuses, brilliant red bougainvillea draped over stone walls and red tile roofs, conveying the same sense of benign untouchability as a cardinal's robes.

Fortson was conscious of his beginnings among the young dreamers who had fled the mind-numbing normalcy of places like Kansas and Nebraska for the mind-numbing party life of sex, booze, Ecstasy and coke. Twenty years ago, he had been an aspiring director straight out of northern Idaho who had slept and bribed and threatened his way to the top of the international film industry.

To the chagrin of every stepping stone he had crushed in his Sherman-like march to success, he was a brilliant director. Many an Oscar presenter had grudgingly forced a smile and handed him another gold statue. At the post-Oscar parties, trampled-on actors, cinematographers, costume designers and party-crashing gofers huddled to commiserate and to plot the perfect means of dispatching Bull Fortson—and then they would make a movie about it. The question was, who would direct?

Fortson had moved from a firetrap motel on Pacific

Coast Highway to a modest house in the Palisades, to an estate in gated Bel Air before he had added his Malibu digs to his property holdings. Somewhere in his migration, he and a minor starlet, Jessica Bennington, had attached themselves to each other like leeches. They married; but, while his career continued to ascend, Fortson was seen more and more without her at celebrity parties and awards ceremonies and with a trophy date on his arm. Sometimes two. Jessica had lost a bit of her press appeal when she picked up a few pounds and a tremor in her hands from her various habits that were as hard to shed as the pounds.

Jessica was still welcome in several quite disparate circles—the wealthy users of Malibu and Bel Air, the sisterhood of other faded stars and the polo crowd of which her husband was a member. She didn't play the game, but her ticket to their genteel circle consisted of the Wolfgang Puck-caliber banquets she catered from the trunk of her Jaguar, the gossip she garnered by listening in on her husband's phone conversations and her repertoire of refreshingly innocent jokes.

"What's black and white and red all over? A zebra that's just found out where zebras come from."

Will Rogers State Park's entrance was as humble as the man himself had been, with the entrance off Sunset on a curve and easily missed. Fortson signaled left and, after the opposing traffic cleared, turned and began the climb along the western edge of a small canyon lined with manzanita, oak, eucalyptus, sycamore and indigenous chaparral, inhabited by a universe of flying and crawling critters that Fortson eyed warily but was determined to ignore.

He continued past a residential area on his left to the park's entrance, where he waved to the park attendant in the tiny booth who collected parking fees from visitors. The polo players were spared such trivia.

On the left was the thirty-one room Rogers house and, above, the stables that looked out on the sweeping expanse of lawn, dotted on this typical June Saturday by picnickers. Looming as a backdrop were the rugged Santa Monica Mountains, teeming with more of Mother Nature's brand of predators. To the right, below the road, was the only remaining outdoor polo field in the Los Angeles area, out of more than thirty in Rogers' day. Fortson felt like aristocracy every time he thought about being a member of the dwindling polo community.

Even though he had eaten a generous lunch, the fragrance of the freshly mowed grass stimulated his appetite, and he thought ahead to the menu he had carefully planned for their anniversary tomorrow. Jessica had been particularly affectionate in recent days—or, more accurately, nights—and a candlelight dinner of filet mignon at home with her favorite, outrageously expensive red wine that he had picked especially for her would fit the bill. She could have her wine all to herself, while he would enjoy a chardonnay. And after the anniversary dinner, well… He smiled. After dinner Bull Fortson's future was an unwritten script.

Jessica was kneeling on a picnic blanket on the grassy margin of the field and pouring champagne refills for the half dozen others gathered around her. Her red hair fluttered in the sunshine like flames. Fortson stopped and leaned across to call to her out the open passenger window, "Jess, honey, I already picked up your special wine, but I'll stop for the steaks on my way home."

She jumped up, exposing her still-stunning legs as she toddled to the car on spindly heels then leaned in for a passionate kiss. "Knock 'em dead!" she said cheerily.

"That's always the plan," he replied and drove on, circling the eastern end of the field to access the corrals on the south side, behind the wood rail fence and scoreboard. Carlos had unloaded Fortson's eight horses from the trailer and had half of them in their tack when Fortson parked his Rolls beside the trailer.

"Damn it, Carlos! What've you been doing all this time, you lazy Mexican?" Fortson gestured toward the other grooms, whose entire strings were in their tack, tails braided and tied up, ankles wrapped in colorful protectors, hooves polished. Fortson was well aware that Carlos was Costa Rican.

The result of the deliberate, insulting rebuke in front of his peers was registered in Carlos' clenched fists and a face that was flushed with suppressed anger. "The truck, it had a fla' coming down."

"Always some excuse," Fortson muttered. He opened the trunk to get his shiny black helmet and heavy leather knee protectors. He was already wearing the traditional white canvas jodhpurs, boots that ended just below the knee, and a black polo shirt with a red number three on the back. His athletic physique, thick, wavy black hair and a perpetual smirk, had seduced many a sweet young thing. And a few not-so-young things, when it paid off.

The four players on each team had their separate assignments, although in the heat of the competition, any player might take over another's role if the other was engaged by the opposition. The numbers one and two were generally the ones to stay forward and therefore more likely to score. Number four's job was to "keep the back door closed," meaning to guard the mouth of the opponent's goal, much like a hockey goalie. The game was, in fact, frequently referred to as hockey on horseback.

That diminutive description totally overlooked the fact that men on half-ton animals wearing iron shoes and moving at thirty miles an hour made it the most dangerous sport in the world. Race car drivers had more protection.

Fortson's teammates had originally been glad to have him on their team because he was competent as well as aggressive. But when he had assigned himself the number three position, they resented having him as team captain, essentially the quarterback, calling all the plays and always taking credit, never giving any in return. A few players knew that Fortson was severely allergic to bee stings and insect bites. Most of them would have gone to a funeral for the bee before they would attend one for Fortson.

He had his fans, however—a couple of players on the opposing team and quite a few spectators. Those afraid to play the game fantasized about doing so in his reckless, daredevil style.

Fortson was conscious of Carlos' angry eyes watching him as he checked each horse that was ready for play. Without even looking at the groom, Fortson said, "I know you've been loosening the cinches between chukkers."

"Oh, no, *jefe*, I no..."

"Shut your damn mouth. I know better. And I don't want you messing with my water bottles, either."

Fortson looked across the dirt drive that went through the corral area and saw Raymond Lincoln in the red shirt of the opposing team strapping on his knee guards. Lincoln was an anomaly, one of the few African-Americans playing polo. Fortson, helmet under one arm, walked over to the tall, slender man and said, "What's this I hear, that you're going to ump an arena polo game?"

"That's right, the celebrity match next Saturday."

Just as Fortson enjoyed goading Carlos, he considered it sport to try raising Lincoln's ire. Fortson smirked. "I'm surprised they'd put any of you in a position of such authority."

Lincoln's mouth dropped open slightly before he replied, with every muscle taut, "Some of us are even licensed to carry a gun."

"Yeah, and I'll bet you wish you were one of them. Don't be so damn sensitive. Polo's always been a white man's sport, and I'm just not used to seeing..."

"...A black who's not mucking out the stalls," Lincoln interrupted tersely. He laid one hand on the back of Fortson's neck. "Polo's a dangerous game, Fortson. Watch your neck out there." His dark eyes narrowed in anger, and he rubbed Fortson's neck harshly several times before Fortson shrugged him off.

Fifteen minutes before the starting time of two o'clock, players and two mounted umpires wearing vertical black and white striped polo shirts cantered onto the field. The players took practice swings at nonexistent balls, allowing their first horse to warm up and them to loosen up their hitting arms.

Finally, the announcer alerted the spectators that the game was about to start. "The players have lined up centerfield at the northern sideline for the umpire's starting throw-in," he began, his voice kicking into overdrive as he continued, "The battle is underway, with both teams fighting for the ball that's somewhere in the tangle of horses' legs!"

The sounds of snorting, stamping horses, growling

players, leather boots and knee protectors squawking against each other rolled up the bank like a gathering wave, accompanied by the sharp clattering of wood mallets competing for the ball.

A player's equipment and horse could cost ten thousand dollars, and every player had a horse for each of the six regulation periods. Most had eight. Doctors, attorneys, an ambassador, an award-winning director and others with mega bucks were risking their lives and a small fortune for possession of a four-inch white plastic ball that cost three bucks.

Bull Fortson's voice boomed over all others. "Mine! Leave it!" he shouted when the ball was knocked free from the cluster of players and out into the open field. He turned his horse hard about with the reins in his left hand, while tethered to his right wrist was the mallet that he used to whack the horse.

Red's number four charged after him and came parallel on Fortson's off side, his right. The red player pulled his mallet across the neck of his horse, leaning down to try to get a near-side back shot away from Fortson's goal. But he couldn't get enough room, so he straightened, pulling the mallet back across to his right and forcing his horse hard to the left, against Fortson's, riding him off the ball.

The Red player gave his teammate a chance to close from behind to take the hit that the first man had wanted. The ball soared in a high arc toward the left goal, and the players turned en masse to charge that direction. Grass and sod flew, and the ground shook as Fortson bellowed orders that his teammates were already executing.

Fortson's one and two players were exactly where they should have been, with number one out front in pursuit of the ball and number two hanging back only enough to ride off an opponent. Black's number one hit an equally effective back shot, sending the ball streaking downfield toward their goal. Fortson anticipated it and turned to go after the ball. His number four was nearer Fortson than the other two, and he rode off Lincoln, who was charging toward the ball.

Fortson was unaware of the defensive move going on behind him. He felt the thundering machine under him and saw only the ball and the blur of the two uprights in the distance.

He was oblivious to the announcer saying excitedly, "Fortson's winding up for an off-side forehand, and he's well within striking distance at twenty yards out!" Fortson's blow sent a loud clack echoing like a gunshot in the warm summer air.

"He hit the ball so hard I thought it was going to set the grass on fire! And the goalie's flag confirms we have our first goal on the board, ladies and gentlemen, one for Team Black, scored by Bull Fortson aboard Headache. I think Fortson might consider renaming his thoroughbred after its splendid performance covering nearly the length of the field twice nonstop at full gallop. For you first-time polo spectators, a regulation field is three times the length of a football field and twice as wide. That's a lot of territory."

The teams switched goals, and an umpire made the throw-in to restart the play. Both teams' horses tore up the sod with their thunderous charging, first in one direction then the other throughout the first three seven-and-half-minute chukkers. At the half, spectators trailed down the slope onto the field for the traditional stomping of divots back into place.

Fortson pulled off his drenched shirt and used a clean towel from his trunk to dry himself. Just as he was about to change into a fresh shirt, he was surprised by the sound of Jessica's voice from behind him. "Let me do that! It's almost as sexy as taking it off."

Fortson was already high from the stimulation of the game, and he was immediately aroused by his wife's suggestive remark. She was swinging her hips and fluffing her fiery tresses as she approached, her glorious cleavage leading the way. He couldn't quite account for her sudden upsurge in interest in the sex department, and he wondered if she had evolved into one of those kinky women who thrived on verbal abuse and rough sex. Well, he could dream, anyway.

Jessica took the shirt from him, embraced his hot body and smothered his mouth with an intense kiss. "For your heroic performance," she said melodramatically and had him bend so that she could slip on the shirt. He was tucking it in when she said, "Oh, your tag's out," and she stood on tiptoe to take hold of the collar, pulling it loose and deliberately tickling his neck before she let go.

"Cut it out, Jess!" he said with a laugh and pulled away. He felt a shiver down his back and guessed that he hadn't dried off all the sweat very well. "Why aren't you stomping divots with your friends?"

"When there's a sexy man half naked within reach?"

Carlos had discreetly turned away when she had embraced her husband. Now he stole a look at the pair and at the grooms and players within hearing who were snickering at her comment.

Raymond Lincoln waited until she had walked away to come over and reach out for Fortson's neck. "Still in one piece, I see," he said, rubbing it roughly.

Fortson slapped Lincoln's hand away and snarled, "It's starting to look like you think I'd make a nice boyfriend."

Lincoln's breath hissed through nostrils flared with rage. "Just watch your damn neck!" he said in a low, menacing voice. "I intend to get back the goal you stole from us."

"What the hell are you talking about?"

"Just that the umps didn't see you throw an elbow into my ribs."

"What a wimp!"

Lincoln shook his head and stalked away. The fact that using elbows was illegal was lost on Fortson. He was energized by his wife's seductive manner, which promised a rousing finish to their evening as well as by the thought of the unlimited and even wilder sexual pleasures available to him after their anniversary. Soon. Only tomorrow.

Fortson was also wound up from his encounter with Lincoln. He was certain that Lincoln dreamed of trampling him to pieces out of jealousy. Lincoln was ranked a goal lower than Fortson's three. Ten goals was the highest rating, and the dozen who achieved it were true polo aristocracy.

Less than three minutes remained in the game when Fortson started to feel on fire. Sweat was raining off him, and his stomach was threatening rebellion. It had been too long since lunch for food poisoning to be likely. And he had drunk only the water from the supply of bottles in the open trunk of his car.

"Take it, Bull! Take it!" he heard his number one call from behind. With reactions so slow that he felt he was in a dream, Fortson lined his horse up with the path of the ball and leaned down to take it at a gallop. The grass seemed to rise up like a sea swell, and he lurched upright and grabbed the front of the saddle with both hands.

Team Red's number four man gave the ball a near-side back shot, sending it down field toward Red's goal; and when the umpire blew the whistle to call a crossing foul, play stopped and Fortson's teammate cantered over. "You all right? You look like hell."

"Think I'm coming down with something."

"You want to go out? We're three up and only two minutes to go."

"I'm not a damn quitter."

But Fortson might as well not have been in the game. He remained dizzy and slow to react, and he was relieved when the horn announced the end of the match. Cantering toward the corral, he felt that he might pass out and fall, so he slowed to a walk.

"*Jefe*," Carlos said with a wrinkled brow, "you don' look so good."

"Feel like hell. What'd you put in the water?"

"*El agua?*" he asked, with his forehead puckered even more.

"Yes, dammit! Made me sick."

"Oh, no, *Señor* Fortson! I don' touch you *agua*." He took the horse as Fortson slid off and stumbled to the rear of his car. With blurred vision, he fumbled for the half-full bottle he had left there. There was only a full one, sealed. He sat on the rear bumper and looked around, shouting, "Where the hell's my water? It was open!"

Lincoln glared at him from across the pathway. Carlos was focused on unsaddling the last horse, and Fortson looked up in surprise to see Jessica running his way.

"Honey, what happened out there? Oh, you look sick!" She put the back of her hand to his forehead. "You're burning up!"

He pushed her aside to vomit.

"Dr. Lincoln!" Jessica called. "Bull's sick. Please come take a look."

Lincoln tossed his second knee protector into the rear of his Mercedes SUV and strode to Fortson, who was breathing heavily, his head down. Carlos and two of Fortson's teammates had gathered as Lincoln reached for Fortson's throat. Fortson slapped his hand aside.

"Don't strangle me!" His voice was weak and desperate.

"The carotid's the best place to check your pulse." Lincoln probed for a second until he found the pulse then looked at his watch. "Twice what it should be. He's got all the symptoms of the flu. Take him home and sponge him down to reduce the fever. Keep up the liquids—soda, Gatorade, juice."

"How long will this last?" she asked.

"With the flu I've been seeing, the fever'll break in a couple of hours, then he'll sleep as long as eighteen hours. He should be all right if you keep him hydrated."

Carlos and the others drifted away as Lincoln helped Fortson into the passenger side of the Rolls. Jessica had the presence of mind to stop at the entrance to let the park employee know that she would have to leave her car at least overnight. The attendant clucked sympathetically at the panting man with his eyes clenched shut. His abdomen had become rigid, nearly paralyzing him with pain.

Jessica drove down the road to Sunset and turned toward PCH. She had given the housekeeper and cook the day off, and now she wondered how she would get Bull inside by herself. It was near four, and the ocean glittered beyond its white hem of surf. Colorful spinnakers on a flotilla of sailboats were ballooned out by the breeze, parading like a flock of roosters.

Jessica was greatly relieved to see the gardener's pickup parked outside the house. Benito was Mexican, small in stature, but he had a blond helper who was more than six feet tall and who played beach volleyball regularly. He had the upper body strength to carry Fortson inside to the master suite.

"What's the matter?" the young man asked Jessica. He wasn't even breathing hard. "Wasted?"

"No, a doctor said it's the flu."

"He's awfully heavy for you to undress. I'd better do it."

"If you'll deal with his boots and pants, I can get his shirt off."

Fortson moaned in pain and cursed as they worked to undress him.

"Hey, man, you'll rest better without all these hot clothes."

Jessica tugged her husband's shirt loose from the waistband in front then waited until the gardener's assistant stripped Fortson down to his jockeys. While he held Fortson's hips up so that he wouldn't roll onto his back again, Jessica pushed the shirt up to his armpit. Then, holding his shirt sleeve from the outside near the knit cuff, she pushed her husband's burning arm through the opening.

She repeated the procedure on the opposite side and instructed her helper to open the window for some air. As he did, she dropped the black shirt into the empty wastebasket near the bed, quickly draping the heavy canvas pants over the top.

"Anything else I can do?" the man asked, turning from the open window and observing the miserable man whose feet were working against the sheets in agony.

"No, thank you. You've been an angel."

"Jess! Jess!" Fortson panted and reached out blindly for her.

"You go on now," she said and walked the gardener to the bedroom door, closing it behind him before returning to the bed.

"Sick!" Fortson cried out feebly, and she could hear the violent rumble in his stomach a second before he threw up on his chest.

She left him to get a couple of washcloths and towels from the master bath. "There, there, Bull, honey. Dr. Lincoln said it's just the flu."

"No, sick, 'lergic!" he rasped.

"Oh, now, no one's allergic to the flu."

"'Lergic to bees, black widows."

"I know, sweetie."

"Can't breathe! Get help!" He reached out for her, but his arm fell back, and his breath grew increasingly ragged.

Patiently she sat on the side of the bed, stroking the cool, damp washcloth across his forehead, trying to ignore the bitter smell of vomit from the other cloth and towel she had used. His breaths were deep, gulping gasps, followed after a few seconds by an exhausted exhalation. The afternoon sun had cast a rainbow through the crystal prism on the windowsill onto the wall above the bed. She watched the rainbow march slowly across the wall like a sundial, measuring the passing of the hour from four to five.

It was five-thirty when she noted the purple around

his lips and found it on his fingers and toes as well. It was longer and longer between his gasps for air, and now they were shallower with every breath. He hadn't uttered a syllable for more than an hour, and so she went downstairs. The security monitor for the front door showed that the gardeners had gone. She went to the kitchen and phoned one of the polo spectators with whom she had agreed to have a drink after the game, to make excuses.

"Oh, no, not serious," she told the woman. "A doctor at polo said it's just the flu. I've been giving him 7-Up, but he just dropped off to sleep, and the doctor said he'll be out till tomorrow. I wouldn't feel right leaving him, though."

She got three cans of 7-Up from the pantry and brought them back to the bedroom. Bull hadn't moved, and his lips and extremities were nearly eggplant in color. She put her cheek by his mouth and waited twenty seconds before there was a faint movement of warm, moist air. She carried the sodas to the bathroom, popped the tops and poured all but part of one down the drain, followed by a full minute of running water.

She carried the cans back to the bedroom and set the two empties beside the wastebasket. The other, partially full can, she set on the night stand. It was six-thirty when she checked again for breath and couldn't detect any. She could find no pulse in his carotid; his pupils were fixed and dilated.

She went downstairs and made herself a chicken sandwich. In the process, she noticed on the counter the bottle of wine that Bull had bought for the anniversary celebration he had planned for tomorrow—her favorite. Jessica glanced longingly at the glorious ruby red color. Any celebration would have to wait. Discretion and patience were called for now. Instead, she ate the sandwich with a glass of sauvignon blanc that she used to wash down a Valium. Only one, she noted with satisfaction. She watched the news on CNN for a couple of minutes, and then she put *Titanic* into the VCR. When it finished, she traded it for *Shakespeare in Love*.

She left the video running and went upstairs at ten-thirty. Bull was quite stiff all over, his body noticeably cooler to the touch, though he was far from cold. From the pocket of her shorts, she extracted a glass jar about two inches in height and diameter. The black metal lid had been punctured a half dozen times with an ice pick.

She was pleased to see that her hands were steady, even under the circumstances. She had found a doctor who was helping her get off pills, helping her regain control over her life.

Gingerly she removed the canvas pants from over the wastebasket. Even more gingerly she removed the black shirt and coaxed the fine specimen of a black widow spider onto a pen before dropping it into the jar and putting the empty soda cans in the wastebasket. She deposited the spider in the dark space behind the small door in the garage wall that gave access to the kitchen pipes. She buried the jar in an empty Grape Nuts box at the bottom of the garbage can.

When the police and paramedics came, near eleven, they found a distraught woman, beating her chest with guilt over falling asleep downstairs while her husband had appeared to be sleeping off the flu.

The paramedics noted the bites on Fortson's back. "Did he complain about feeling any bites?" one of them asked.

Jessica frowned. "That's strange—no."

"Not so strange, actually. Quite often, the bite is not felt at all. I think you said that your husband was in a polo match just before he exhibited flu-like symptoms."

"Yes, why?"

"Well, it would explain why he didn't notice the bites and why he didn't realize he was in trouble. But I was wondering how a black widow got inside his shirt."

"There are loads of spiders and insects where he parks, and his shirt was in the trunk, open, when he changed at the half."

"Ah, perfectly understandable, then."

* * *

The death of Bull Fortson was a loss to the film industry and a source of relief to the many he had abused, Jessica and Raymond Lincoln among them. While many expected Bull's death to send Jessica on a downward spiral, it did the opposite. Raymond Lincoln had been the one to wean her off her various dependencies, and her career was rekindled.

Jessica and Raymond married quietly one evening in his Bel Air home eleven months after Fortson's death. After the guests had gone, the newlyweds shared a very expensive bottle of red wine—Jessica's favorite, a friend later told the press. The bottle contained a quick-acting poison, and they were found in the master suite. It was declared an inexplicable double suicide. Only Bull Fortson would have known otherwise.

We've reached the end of the road, and just in time: the sun has all but disappeared into the horizon over the Pacific, casting a wide, golden beam over the surface of the water, a bridge of light that leads straight toward us, transforming the entire western sky into a beautiful mosaic of blue, orange and pink.

Our journey is over. Hopefully, you've enjoyed the ride. From here you can go north up the coast highway, and stop in at the site of the café and gambling club owned by 1930s screen siren Thelma Todd, whose death from asphyxiation in her nearby garage is one of L.A. longest officially-unsolved mysteries. Or you can go south to Santa Monica Bay, under whose waters the remains of gambling equipment from the Rex and other mob-owned floating casinos (and perhaps even the remains of a few gamblers) still lie hidden.

Of course, you could always turn around and hitch a ride back up Sunset. There are more neighborhoods to be explored—more sights, more shops, more places of interest.

Even more stories...

AUTHOR BIOGRAPHIES

DANA KOUBA is the pseudonym of S. Dana Stiebel, a Los Angeles attorney, real estate executive, and former rough carpenter engaged in a thirty-year love affair with old buildings, historic urban neighborhoods and the unlikely mix of characters they attract. She is currently circulating her supernatural mystery novel, *The Water Strider*, among agents and editors.

GAYLE McGARY is a painter and sculptor as well as a writer. Her previous short stories were published in Sisters in Crime/L.A.'s anthologies, *Murder by Thirteen* and *A Deadly Dozen*. Gayle teaches art in Los Angeles and lives in nearby Altadena with her husband, writer Richard Partlow.

RICHARD PARTLOW's stories have appeared in *Rod Serling's Twilight Zone* magazine. He has worked as a librarian with the Los Angeles Public Library, as manager of several Central Library subject departments, including the Central/Southern region of 13 branches. He is currently working on a mystery novel.

DALE FURUTANI has been called "a master craftsman" by *Publishers Weekly* and "the best known of Japanese American authors" by *Nikkei View*. He has won an Anthony and a Macavity award, and has been nominated for an Agatha. He has also earned honors outside the mystery field, including speaking at the Library of Congress and being named one of the "44 Faces of Diversity" for the City of Los Angeles. He has written modern and historical mysteries, including the *L.A. Times* bestseller *Kill the Shogun, Death in Little Tokyo, The Toyotomi Blades, Death at the Crossroads* and *Jade Palace Vendetta.* Dale and his wife currently live in Tokyo, Japan, where he is working on a new book.

JOAN WAITES has a degree in Chemistry with a focus in Forensic Science. She was recently awarded first prize for fiction in the San Diego Writer's Cooperative Contest, and her work has appeared, under a pseudonym, in the *San Diego Writer's Journal.*

KATE THORNTON has published short stories in a variety of magazines, including *Blue Murder, Murderous Intent Mystery Magazine, Woman's World, The Cozy Detective,* as well as in the anthologies *A Deadly Dozen* and *The Best of Blue Murder.* Twice nominated for a Derringer Award by the Short Mystery Fiction Society, she has also published extensively in the science-fiction genre.

GAY TOLTL KINMAN has published over 100 magazine articles. Her story, "Miss Parker and the Cutter-Sanborn Tables," which appeared in *A Deadly Dozen,* was nominated for an Agatha Award at Malice Domestic. Her middle reader title, *The Mystery of the Missing Miniature Books,* was a finalist for the Independent E-Book Awards and has been reprinted in a trilogy with *The Mystery of the Octagon House* and *The Mystery of the Missing Arabian.* She co-edited *Desserticide II* aka *Just Desserts and Deathly Advice.* Her play, *The Wicked Well,* was produced in Cambria, a town that lays in the shadow of Hearst Castle, which is the setting for her gothic novel, *Castle Reiner.*

MAE WOODS is a writer-producer whose screenplay credits include three episodes of HBO's offbeat series *Tales from the Crypt*. She produced the TV movie *When Danger Follows You Home* for USA Networks. She was the development executive for Walter Hill's production company for four years and associate producer on *Streets of Fire, Brewster's Millions, Crossroads, Extreme Prejudice, Red Heat* and *Johnny Handsome*. She co-edited *Murder by Thirteen*, SinC/L.A.'s debut anthology. Her freelance writing credits include stints at Mysterynet and Digital City.

LINDA O. JOHNSTON's first published story, "Different Drummers," appeared in *Ellery Queen's Mystery Magazine* and won the Robert L. Fish Memorial Award for Best First Mystery Short Story of the Year. It was anthologized in *The Year's Best Mystery and Suspense Stories* for 1989. Since then, Linda has had several more short stories published, plus nine romance novels, including *Operation: Reunited, Marriage: Classified*, and *Alias Mommy*.

PAUL D. MARKS's story "Santa Claus Blues" was nominated for a Pushcart Prize. Another of his stories, "Netiquette," won first place in the *Futures* Short Story Contest. He has also sold stories to *Dogwood Tales, Futures, Penny-A-Liner* and other publications. "Angels Flight" appeared in the anthology *Murder by Thirteen*. Paul is a stealth screenwriter, making his living from optioning screenplays of his own and rewriting (script doctoring) other people's scripts or developing their ideas. He has also lectured on writing and screenwriting at UCLA, California State University, San Bernadino, Learning Tree University and at other seminars or conferences. A Los Angeles native, he loves the city that

L.A. was. Dodging bullets, he's not so sure about the city it is today. He is currently at work on a mystery novel.

ANNE RIFFENBURGH is a medical social worker who found that ten years in the field of medical social work came in handy in writing "Leap of Faith," her first short mystery story. Anne is the author of *The Power of Reminiscence* and *Grandparents and Grandkids: A Celebration of Love*, and her essay "The Race" appears in *Chicken Soup for the Nurses Soul.*

GABRIELLA DIAMOND is the pseudonym of Linda Lane McCall, who adopted the pen name "Gabriella Diamond" to distinguish her books that feature the game of polo along with an equal dose of romance and suspense. Her novels *On the Run* and *Tapping at the Window* have been published by Pocket Books. Her story "Lust for Life" won the Writers' Forum Short Story Prize in the fall of 2001 and another tale, "Allies," was the Grand Prize Winner in the 2001-2002 short story contest sponsored by SunnySide Up Publications. In the words of her editor at greatUNpublished.com: "What [Dick] Francis has done for horseracing, Gabriella Diamond is doing for polo."

EDITOR BIOGRAPHIES

ROCHELLE KRICH has been noted by former *L.A. Times* reviewer Charles Champlin for her "superior crime fiction." Rochelle won the Anthony for *Where's Mommy Now?*, filmed as *Perfect Alibi*. In addition to her suspense novels (*Speak No Evil, Fertile Ground*), she writes the Agatha Award-nominated series starring Jessica Drake, "one of the more intriguing detectives in the field" (*Publishers Weekly*). The series (*Fair Game, Angel of Death, Blood Money, Dead Air,* and *Shadows of Sin*) has been optioned for film. *Romantic Times* has nominated *Dead Air* for Best Novel, and the author herself for Career Achievement in suspense. *Blues in the Night,* introducing true crime writer and freelance reporter Mollie Blume, will be published by Ballantine in October 2002. Her Agatha-nominated short story, "Widow's Peak" (*Unholy Orders,* Intrigue Press), has also been nominated for an Anthony.

MICHAEL MALLORY has published some seventy short stories in such magazines and anthologies as *Murderous Intent, Crimestalker Casebook, The Strand, Over My Dead Body!, Blue Murder, Mysterynet.com, The Mammoth Book of Legal Thrillers* and the upcoming *Our Sherlock Holmes,* from St. Martin's. His story "Curiosity Kills" won a Derringer Award from the Short Mystery Fiction Society. He is the author of *The Adventures of the Second Mrs. Watson,* a collection of interconnected stories; *Hanna-Barbera Cartoons,* which was selected by *People Magazine* as a 1998 "Holiday Pick;" and *Marvel: The Characters and Their Universe.* A former show writer for Disneyland, Michael is also a freelance journalist, covering film and animation for the *Los Angeles Times* and *Animation Magazine.*

LISA SEIDMAN was a co-editor on the first Sisters in Crime/L.A. mystery anthology, *Murder by Thirteen.* On television, she's written for *Cagney & Lacey, Dallas, Knots Landing, Murder, She Wrote* and currently writes for the daytime soap *Guiding Light.* Her short story, "Over My Shoulder," was published in the second SinC/L.A. anthology, *A Deadly Dozen.* She also teaches screenwriting at UCLA Extension where she was honored as Teacher of the Year in 2000.

Author Copyrights